DeCoys, INC.

SHONDA CHEEKES

SBi

STREBOR BOOKS

NEW YORK LONDON TORONTO SYDNEY

SBI

Strebor Books
P.O. Box 6505
Largo, MD 20792
http://www.streborbooks.com

ISBN 978-1-59309-206-1
ISBN 978-1-4165-8506-0 (e-book)
LCCN 2008933588

First Strebor Books trade paperback edition October 2008

Cover design: www.mariondesigns.com
Cover photograph: © Keith Saunders/Marion Designs

10 9 8 7 6 5 4 3 2 1

Manufactured in the United States of America

For information regarding special discounts for bulk purchases, please contact Simon & Schuster Special Sales at 1-866-506-1949 or business@simonandschuster.com

The Simon & Schuster Speakers Bureau can bring authors to your live event. For more information or to book an event, contact the Simon & Schuster Speakers Bureau at 1-866-248-3049 or visit our website at www.simonspeakers.com.

To my daughter, Calina—
for pushing me to keep going when I wanted to give up.

CHAPTER 1

"Deeva, it's not personal. We're going through a tough time right now, with the economy being the way it is and all."

The more Evan talked, the louder the ringing in my ears seemed to get..

"We haven't taken on any new accounts in months."

Was he kidding me? Did he suddenly forget I was the one responsible for setting up any new files that came through the door, fax, or computer? I'd done three of them the previous week alone.

"If business picks up we'll—"

"Evan, don't waste your time. Better yet, don't waste mine. You think business has slowed down? Wait until I let all of my contacts know how you tried to bamboozle me. You're about to find out what slowed down really means."

"Deeva, there's no need to—"

"No, Evan, there was no need for you to attempt to force feed me this bullshit excuse. I've been at this company for five years. For five years, Evan, I've sat patiently by and watched everyone else get promoted. I listened to you, when you told me to wait; that my time was coming. I remained loyal to you and *your* company. Helped you bring in new business." By then, I was on my feet, my anger having propelled me from my seat. I pulled at the different things I'd brought in to personalize my space over the years and threw them in the box.

"Deeva, as I said earlier, this was not an easy decision for me to make."

"Really, Evan? Then why is it that I seem to be the only person being let go?"

Evan tried to divert his eyes from my face.

"Exactly! Don't think I'm going to go away quietly either. Expect a call from my lawyer."

The look of fear on Evan's face was payment enough; even though I'd never let him know it. Not one for confrontation with the proper authorities, Evan realized I had enough dirt to bury his ass more than the suggested six feet. Surely my severance package would be laced with a lil' something extra, once we worked it out.

I sat in my car for a few minutes, wondering what my next move should be.

"A letter of recommendation? He can shove that shit where the sun don't shine." I angrily shoved the key into the ignition.

A few hours later, the girls arrived at my home to participate in my pity party.

"Damn, Deeva," Cara said. "I can't believe his black ass would do you like that. You practically helped Evan build his business. Now he wants to go in a different direction? What the hell is that supposed to mean?"

Before I could reply, Ebonee chimed in. "I'll tell you what it means, Cara."

"What does is it mean, Eb?"

By now, we were all a bit on the tipsy side.

"It means his blacker than Wesley Snipes ass wants to have Becky's ass as the face of his business now."

"The face of his business?" Cara asked.

"Yes. She'll be the first face people see when they walk through the door. Right now Deeva's face—even though it's not as dark as his—is a bit too brown for the caliber of clientele he's going after."

"It's not like Deeva's ghetto or something," Lisa slurred.

"Being ghetto has nothing to do with it," Eb continued. "Deeva puts the 'P' in professional but, at the end of the day, what people see is what matters to some folks."

"And, on that note, I'd like to raise my glass," I said, my words slightly slurred.

Cara, Ebonee, and Lisa all raised their glasses; each looking at me expectantly as they waited for my next words.

"This one is for you guys." I nodded my head toward them. "Thank you for having my back. For dropping everything and rushing right over; with bottles in hand, I might add."

They all laughed.

My eyes began to tear up and my voice caught in my throat. I had to get my emotions in check before I could continue.

"Hey, hey, now. We got you, girl. Don't you ever forget that." Cara reached over and hugged me. The rest followed suit.

My nowhere job had ended but, without somewhere else to go, I felt lost. I had to figure out something, but what?

CHAPTER 2

The next two weeks went by in a blur of nothing. I did nothing. Pretty much ate nothing. The couch was starting to get a groove in it from the countless hours I'd spent sitting in the same spot in front of "the idiot box," as my dad affectionately called the television.

The Mandrel Polk Show had become my favorite pastime. I especially loved the episodes where he would hire what he called "Sexy Decoys" to help prove whether or not a man was cheating.

Without fail, every man went for the bait and ended up getting caught on tape trying to hook up with the decoy. After this was shown, I didn't know why he even wasted time reading the results of the polygraph tests the assholes volunteered to take. Obviously, he enjoyed adding more nails to their coffins.

I was able to get more than my fill of daily drama since the show aired three times a day.

"Girl, when was the last time you ventured outside?" Cara turned up her nose as she maneuvered around a pile of clothes; one of many strewn throughout my house.

"I've been outside. I go out to get my mail every day." I pointed to the stack of unopened mail on the entryway table.

"You seriously need to reconnect with those of us in the living world. We're taking you out tonight, and don't think about telling me no. That's not an option."

"Whatever!" I patted the cushion underneath me. "I'm fine sitting right here."

Cara pulled out her cell phone and started pressing buttons. "Umm, hmm, girl. She's sitting in the same spot. Oh, I told her. Okay. I'll see you when you get here. Bye."

"Come on now. There's nothing wrong with me. I don't need to go out…"

"I'll be in your room finding you something to wear. I'll turn on the shower so the water'll be warm enough for you to get in." Without another word, she walked into my bedroom.

I threw my head back and breathed deeply. There was no use in fighting her, so I did as I was told.

"Now aren't you glad you came?" Cara yelled over the loud music of the live band.

We ended up at a trendy spot in Atlanta, well known for its delicious food and first-rate entertainment. Two Urban Licks was nestled in a warehouse district, but that didn't stop people from coming out. The valet line was backed up to the street when we pulled in. Your best bet was to call ahead and make a reservation, if you didn't want to spend at least an hour waiting.

I swayed to the smooth sounds of the jazz quartet. The atmosphere was a nice change from sitting in front of the blue light of my television. My stomach was sure to express gratitude for getting a break from the microwave meals.

"I don't believe this," Ebonee stated as she watched her ex walk in.

We all looked at one another and burst into a chorus of laughter.

Willie Walker had been the love of Ebonee's life during our days at Clark Atlanta University. Every single day for three years straight, we were sure to see him or hear his name.

"I haven't seen that fool in like, forever. Since I kicked his ass out, after we set his ass up. Deeva, you remember that?"

"Umm, hmm." Boy, did I ever remember it.

"Willie's no good ass is at it again." Ebonee stormed into my room and flopped down on the bed.

"What has he done this time?" I asked in a lackluster tone.

For far too long, Ebonee had been going through the

same drama with Willie. I was sick and tired of constantly hearing about it. Like clockwork, Willie did something every other Friday to upset her. She'd sit around moping all weekend, while he went out and enjoyed himself. It was all a ploy. By pissing her off, he didn't have to worry about her drilling him with questions while he did his dirt.

"Nothing you want to hear about—again."

"I'm glad you know this." I smacked my lips together, after applying a nice even coat of lipstick.

"I don't think I'm going to go tonight." Ebonee sighed as she played with the floppy ears of the stuffed animal on my queen-sized bed.

"Damn, Ebonee! You do this every weekend." I turned from the mirror to face her.

"Do what?"

I gave her a look that spoke volumes.

"I know, Deeva, but he's got my head all…all…"

"Screwed up! While you're here worrying about Willie, he's out getting his jollies off." *More than likely with someone else*, I wanted to add, but she was my girl and I couldn't be that cruel.

She rolled over on her back and stared at the ceiling. "When I ask him if he's cheating on me…"

If sound effects could have been added, the sound of a needle being dragged across a record would have been appropriate at that moment. I stared at her in disbelief.

"Ask him? Are you serious? You actually think he's

going to tell you the truth? Girl, please. Your ass is stuck on stupid or something."

"What do you suggest I do then, Deeva?" The attitude in her voice almost caused me to cuss her out, but I decided to do one better.

"I *suggest* you do a lil' research of your own. Set his ass up and see if he falls for the bait."

This made Ebonee sit up.

"Set him up how?"

"Since he knows me, it's out of the question for me to do it, but I have a cousin who dances at a club. We can have her approach him and see what he does."

"You think she'll do it?"

"Think? I know she will."

The questionable look on her face told me she wanted a little bit of back history.

"We've done it before. I've done it for her and she's done it for me. So, it's not a question as to whether she'll do it. The only question at stake is if you *want* us to do it."

I could tell she was thinking hard. We all have that "need to know" cell in our DNA that takes control every now and then. But, at the same time, we wonder if we're ready for what we may find.

"Exactly what are you going to do?"

I began to explain it to her in a controlled tone. "My cousin will approach him and act like she's interested. If he tries to holla at her, then you'll have your answer. If he doesn't, guess that means he's telling you the truth and maybe things aren't as bad as you think they are."

Ebonee processed this information a while longer before agreeing to give it a try. It was on from there.

I called my cousin LaNasha and set everything up for the following night. Despite Ebonee's protest, I was able to get her to go out that night and enjoy herself.

"I'm going to ask you one more time. Are you sure you want to go through with this?" I turned in my seat to face Ebonee, who was sitting in the backseat of my car.

She shrugged her shoulders. "We're here now."

"Okay." I turned to LaNasha and told her how our little plan was going to go down. After the five-minute briefing, LaNasha got out of the car and walked into the club. Finding Willie would not be a problem. It was his Saturday night haunt and his car was parked in the lot. She would be able to roll up on him in his favorite hold up spot—near the bar in the rear of the club.

"Do we have to go in?" Ebonee asked.

"You don't have to. On the other hand, I'm going in, just in case Nasha has a problem."

I waited the planned ten minutes and got out of the car, leaving Ebonee staring out of the window.

It was Ladies Night so there was no cover. I showed my ID and then eased into the semi-crowded club. Midnight was still considered early for the club scene, but a special performance was scheduled. No one wanted to take the chance and miss the opportunity to rub elbows with some of the hottest acts in the industry.

I spotted LaNasha, who had wasted no time in finding Willie. She had gotten him away from his crew and he had her hemmed up in the corner. He hovered an inch away from her ear. Playing the part, LaNasha was laughing it up for him, batting her eyelashes and touching him any chance she got. It was all a part of the act. If we were going to nail him in one shot, she had to flirt and flirt hard.

We'd been in the club for almost an hour when I felt we'd gotten him hooked enough to bust his ass. I took out my cell phone and called Ebonee. She let it ring four times before she answered.

"Well?"

"Well? You need to come in here so we can tie this thing up."

"Tie it up?!" she exclaimed.

"It's a done deal, girl. I hate to tell you this, but…" I paused. Ebonee prided herself on their three-year relationship.

"I'm on my way in right now."

She disconnected the call before I could respond. I looked toward the entrance in time enough to see her charging through the crowd.

"Not like that, Ebb," I said to myself. She was running on pure emotions. I had to think fast or I was going to find myself in the middle of a scene that went from intense to insane in the blink of an eye. I jumped up and met her before she got close enough for Willie to see her.

"Ebonee, you've got to be cool about this, or you're going to come off looking like a fool. Not to mention, you're going to be putting my cousin out there like that and I'm not about to let that happen." I snatched her by the arm and ushered her into the bathroom.

"Be cool?! Are you serious?!"

"Dead ass serious. Look, if you go over there half-cocked, ready to go upside his head, you'll ridicule yourself. Then, he'll know he's got you. But, if you go over there and speak cool and calmly, in the friendliest tone you have, that's going to rattle his cage. He won't know what to think."

"He's in there all over another chick and you want me to play nice?"

"Exactly!"

Ebonee cooled down a bit from the raging bull I'd pulled in a few moments earlier.

"Ebonee, you've got to trust me on this. I've never steered you wrong, in all of our years of friendship. I'm not going to start now."

She gave me a long, hard look and I could see her eyes softening a bit.

"Okay, Deeva. We'll do this your way. But if he comes out his face wrong, I can't promise you what I'll do."

"Cool. Now, let's go wrap this deal up."

We both readjusted our clothing and checked our images in the mirror before going back into the darkened club. We were strictly about business now as we approached Willie, who was close enough to LaNasha to be an extra limb.

LaNasha glanced up and gave us a quick wink before easing back slightly from an unsuspecting Willie.

"Willie? Is that you?" Ebonee asked.

He jerked his head so hard and quick, I thought for sure he had pulled a muscle in it.

"Eb...Ebonee?" His eyes were as big as Chris Tucker's in *Rush Hour*.

"I thought that was you." She leaned in and hugged him. "And you are?" she asked LaNasha, as if she had never seen her before.

"Candy," LaNasha said and reached out for Ebonee's hand.

"Nice to meet you, Candy." Ebonee turned her attention back to Willie. "Well, I see you're busy and all right now, so I'll talk with you later. Enjoy the rest of your night."

You could've blown Willie over with a feather; the way he stood there watching as Ebonee and I walked away from him. His mind must have been going a mile a minute, trying to figure out what was going to happen once he got in later.

"Is he still looking?"

I turned around and waved.

"He's got a beam on you, girl." We both laughed as we pushed our way to the middle of the dance floor and danced as if we didn't have a care in the world.

Just as predicted, Willie's fear of the unknown made him leave the club earlier than usual. By the time Ebonee arrived home, he was pretending to be fast asleep. Not wanting to set Ebonee off, he got up early and came in late two nights in a row. His inability to discuss the matter with Ebonee made her realize he was never going to change. When he came home on the third day, he was shocked to find the locks changed and all of his belongings sitting outside the door in two huge black garbage bags.

"You were always good at stuff like that. You and your cousin."

"Speaking of, where is LaNasha now?" Ebonee asked as she brought her attention back to the table.

"She's working over at Magic City."

"Oh damn! She always said she was about stacking her paper."

"She's stacking paper, all right. If she could only stop spending it as fast as she makes it, maybe her stack would be big enough for her to afford to buy a place and stop renting." I took another sip of my drink.

"What are you talking about?"

"Nasha told me, on a slow night, she can pull in anywhere from seven hundred to maybe a grand. On a good night, *please*. She rarely brings home less than twenty-five hundred."

"Twenty-five hundred! Girl, I know some people who don't make that in a month! I'd work two days a week and chill the other five," Lisa replied.

"Hell, twenty-five hundred in one night? I need to hire me a personal trainer," Ebonee added. We all laughed.

While Ebonee tipped the scales at a little bit more than 200 pounds, she definitely carried it well. Without sounding cliché, she was one of those "beautiful voluptuous women." Regardless to what the media tries to peddle us, brothas love a sistah with meat on her bones. Ebonee was living proof of that.

"But that's what I'm talking about. Most of these girls who dance, they ride around in nice cars. Dress in designer clothes. Carry designer bags, but don't even own a house, a condo, nothing. They usually have nothing more than a night's pay in the bank."

"I wasn't making that kind of loot on my lil' piece of job, but I was still able to put away a decent amount of cash. Imagine how much I would have if I had the balls—" I said.

"I don't think those would work in that particular line of work," Cara quickly corrected me.

"You're so right." We all laughed. "If I had the courage to take my clothes off for a living, and had put the amount of time in that Nasha has, puh-lease. I'd have no less than a cool mil stashed away. My car would be paid off and so would my townhouse."

"I hear ya, girl." Lisa reached up to slap hands with me.

"For the majority of those girls, it's easy come, easy go money." Ebonee shook her head. "Just like niggahs who sell drugs."

Willie walked over to our table. "Hello, strangers." He flashed us a smile.

"Hey to you, too," Ebonee replied.

"Been a long time, Ebby Baby."

"You still remember my name, so I guess it hasn't been long enough." She rolled her eyes and turned away from him.

"Damn, girl, you still feisty as ever. Plus, I see you still holding on to old stuff."

"What can we do for you, Willie Walker?" I asked.

"Damn, a niggah can't come and say hello?" He looked directly at Ebonee.

Cara glared at him. "Okay, you've said it. Now you can move along. You're kinda messing up the vibe we had going."

"I see Cara is still the mouthpiece for the group."

"Yep. That's me. Now move along, Deputy Dog."

"Willie. Willie."

We all turned our attention in the directions of the voice.

"It was nice seeing you ladies again," Willie replied, about to rush off.

"You're not going to introduce us to your friend?" Ebonee turned completely around in her seat so she could get a good look. With the broadest smile plastered on her face, she waved at the woman and gestured for her to come over to our table.

"Ebonee, leave them alone," Lisa pleaded. She was the one in the group who hated any type of conflict.

"Ebonee? Man, what you doing?" Willie asked as he began to back away from our table.

"I'm not doing anything but showing the girl a little Southern hospitality. You know, let her in on the kind of game her man is tryna' run." She smiled a bit brighter as the girl hesitantly came toward the table.

"Crazy ass," Willie mumbled as he finally got around our chairs.

"What's wrong, Willie? All we wanted to do was speak to your lil' girlfriend."

"All right, Ebonee. We're not in that type of establishment," Lisa reminded her.

"Sorry, Lisa. I was starting to forget myself there for a minute."

"Besides, you're making it seem like you've still got feelings for him. I hope that's not the case."

"Girl, now I'm about to show out for real, but on yo' ass. Willie Walker could fall off the face of the earth for all I care. Care about him? I simply wanted to warn her. Wish somebody would've warned me. Deeva, why don't you go offer her your services?"

I laughed.

"Okay, Ebonee. That sounds like a plan."

The rest of the night was lively once we got beyond the Willie scene.

As we stood at the valet stand waiting on my SUV, the woman who'd been with Willie earlier came out the door.

"Excuse me," she said to no one in particular.

I shot Ebonee a look, warning her to behave, but she knew I would throw down for her if it came down to it.

"I wanted to let you ladies know I wasn't upset about Willie coming over to speak to you. He told me he went to college with ya'll." Her body language said she was a bit on the nervous side. As if she was expecting one of us to tell her something different.

"Yes, we all went to school together," Lisa replied.

"Oh, okay. Umm, well, it was nice—"

"Look, I'm Ebonee. I'm not sure how much information Willie has given you about his past, but we dated for about three years. If you ever want to know why we broke up, give me a call." Ebonee passed her a business card.

"We're about to get married, so I don't see why that would be necessary."

"Oh, so you're about to get married? Maybe you should give her your card, then, Deeva. If she know like I do."

"Okay. The car is here." Lisa hurried to the front, where the valet was still pulling up. She grabbed Ebonee's arm on the way.

"Why would I need her number?" the woman asked.

"Listen, we wish you and Willie the best," I replied. "Honestly. But if Willie Walker is anything like he used to be, all I can say is buyer beware."

"Thanks to her..." Ebonee pointed toward me. "I didn't make the mistake you're about to and I got a feeling you know what's up, too." Ebonee climbed into the back of the truck.

As I walked to the driver's side and handed the valet a tip, she walked over to me.

"Do you have a card?"

Stunned into silence, I stared at her blank face for a minute.

"Umm... I don't have any cards on me right now—"

"Well, I'll write your number on the back of her card."

Cara reached over from the front seat and passed her a slip of paper.

"Here's her name, number, and email address."

"Thanks," she said as she began to back away from me.

"Felicia."

"No, I'm Deeva."

"No. My name. It's Felicia. That way you'll know when I call. Felicia," she said again, as she looked down at the paper once more before placing it inside her purse.

"Okay, Felicia."

She gave us a meek wave before heading back inside through the heavy glass doors.

CHAPTER 3

"Girl, you've always been good at it. Why not get paid? You already have your first client." Cara placed her feet on the matching ottoman in front of the leather chair she was sitting on. I was sitting at my desk.

Felicia had called me the very next day, with full details of Willie's comings and goings. Along with that, she gave me a comprehensive story of their rocky one-year romance. The fact that he had proposed after she caught him talking to a woman he claimed that he worked with was enough to get her to thinking after running into us that night. She'd threatened to leave him and put him out of her house. It wasn't the first time he'd been caught.

We scheduled everything to go down the following weekend. She'd told him she was going out of town on business. She wanted to see how much playing the mouse was going to do while the cat was away.

"Let me see the check again." Cara put out her hand. I handed it to her.

"Five hundred American dollars, baby. That's a nice

payment for something that may only take what? An hour at the most? Not even that long, knowing Willie."

"The only thing I need to do now is find someone to do it. It's not like I can use Nasha again."

"If Willie is as dumb as he used to be, yes, you can."

"Cara, that's not nice."

"No, it's not, but it's true." We both laughed.

"Maybe Nasha can ask one of the girls she works with."

"Now, that's an idea. I'll give her a buck fifty and she won't have to take off a stitch of clothing."

"That should be an added plus."

I called Nasha to set everything up.

"Deeva, I can't thank you enough," Felicia said, sipping on a glass of wine. "That five hundred was money well-spent."

I grinned. "Glad I could be of service to you, Felicia."

"Would you mind if I give a friend of mine your number? She's been trying to catch her man for years, but he's been a bit of a slickster. I told her about you and she's willing to pay twice as much as I did."

I was definitely fine with that. A thousand dollars would be really nice.

"Sure. She can give me a call first thing next week."

"I'll let her know."

"Girl, you should've seen Willie's face when I popped in that DVD in front of everyone."

I almost choked on my glass of wine.

"You showed everyone?"

"At the engagement party. I'm thinking about putting it up on YouTube, as a warning for any woman who may come across him in the future."

Willie would probably want to kill me if he knew I had something to do with his demise—*again*.

Felicia held her glass up toward Ebonee. "Thanks, Ebonee. I could've taken your actions as being that of a jealous ex, but something told me it was more to it."

"Girl, I don't want to see another sistah go through what I did."

"More of us should feel that way." Felicia raised her glass to her lips. "I keep saying we need to have more of a sistah-hood with one another. Like women from back in the day."

"You mean back when they would raise one another's children if need be?" I thought about how many children MaDear had raised on those principles. How many uncles and aunts I had who were actually a cousin?

"Well, this was well worth it." Felicia handed me another check. "I wanted to give you a lil' somethin' extra. My mother said to tell you it's a thank you from her."

The one-fifty I paid Nasha's friend was given back to me with interest.

Felicia placed her empty glass on the table. "As much as I'm enjoying this, I really need to get going. Thanks again, Deeva. I'll definitely be sending some business your way." She winked at me.

"Thank you, Felicia," I responded as I looked over the check in my hand.

Everyone waited for her to leave before running over to see how much she'd given me.

"Another five hundred dollars?" Cara asked in amazement.

"Maybe you need to charge more," Ebonee said as she took the check from me.

Maybe I should.

CHAPTER 4

"I was thinking about calling it something catchy."

"Hmm. Let me think." Cara acted as if she was putting on her thinking cap.

"What about Loves P.I.?"

"Ebonee, please. Don't you see I'm tryna' think over here."

She was definitely right about that. Cara was the creative and crafty one of the bunch.

"Give me a pen and a piece of paper." She snapped her fingers. Excitement showed in her eyes.

"Here," Ebonee said as she flung the paper and pen at her.

"Stop being a hater. It's not becoming." She picked up the needed tools and began to write a few things. After a minute she put down the pen and held the paper up.

"Well? Are you going to show us or not?" I was anxious to see what she had come up with.

"Ebonee, come. You look first."

Ebonee walked over and stood behind her.

"Oh yeah! That's hot, Cara!"

"You see how I came up with it."

"That's what makes it hot. "

Not able to stand any more of the growing suspense, I got up and grabbed the paper.

"Damn, you didn't have to snatch it. Didn't your mama teach you some manners?" Cara said.

"Shut up." I sat on the sofa and crossed my legs beneath me.

There on the paper was the perfect name for my business: *DeCoys, Inc.*

"My first and last name blended. That is hot, Cara."

"The smile on your face says it all. Now you just have to get somebody to do a logo for you, print up some business cards, and do a website."

"You know I can help you find a nice office space. You're definitely going to need that." Ebonee took the sheet of paper back from me.

"You know people are going to want to be able to see if you're legit; especially when they're shelling out that kind of money," Lisa said. "You've got to look the part."

"I know that's right, Lisa."

"Well, Ebonee, you know my budget is a bit limited right now. I have to be able to survive off of the money I have in the bank, while I try to get this off the ground."

"Don't put that out into the universe. Think positive and claim it, if you want it."

"I understand that, Ebonee, but you know I'm about my bank account."

"Haven't you ever heard, you gotta spend money to make money?"

The thought of going into my savings was frightening. With no other source of income coming in at the moment, I was afraid of what would happen if things didn't work out.

Cara sat down next to me.

"Look, girl, you have to be willing to gamble on yourself. Everyone else can see your potential. Now it's time for you to open your eyes, so you can see it, too." She stroked my arm for added measure.

By now Lisa and Ebonee had joined us. Each one of them gave me a hug in a show of support and confidence.

"If you need a little something to help tide you over, you know I got you," Ebonee added.

"Yeah, 'cause you know us other folks ain't pulling in the dollars like this top earner Realtor over here." Cara playfully brushed Ebonee's shoulders off.

"Speak for yourself. Unlike you, I have a steady paycheck," Lisa said.

Cara responded, "Lisa, please. Your *paycheck* is nothing like the checks Ebb is getting."

"But I have one, Cara."

"What? So, I'm in between jobs right now. When I'm ready, I'll find another one. Come to think of it, Deeva, you're going to need an administrative assistant. So how about it?"

Cara did have a valid point and she was a really good

candidate, too. With all the temping she'd done over the years, she had more than enough experience and knew how to run an office.

"You have to show up on time."

"I'll be early."

"Right now I can't pay you much, but once business picks up, I'll make sure your pay is more than generous."

"I'll take it!"

"Now that that's settled, let's hear you claim your success." Ebonee reached out for us to join her.

With a slight amount of doubt, I took a deep cleansing breath. "This is for me and I know I'm going to be very successful."

CHAPTER 5

This will be a perfect fit for you," Ebonee said as she passed me the information packet. "The monthly rent includes everything. Lights, water, phones, and internet service." She pulled out her cell phone.

"I have a friend who works for a company that gets furniture from companies that have gone out of business. I'll talk to her and she'll give you a good deal. You need something to start out with. You know, nothing too fancy."

I looked at Ebonee and smiled. She was all business during the week before 5 pm. She didn't believe in being successful by luck. She constantly said it was all about the hustle. This is what set her apart from other real estate agents and she had a slew of awards to prove it.

"I've negotiated for you to get so much toward the build-out of the space."

"Build-out?"

"You're going to want to go in and change a few things. Maybe make the space you choose as your office to be bigger. Move a few walls or something. Give it the feel you want."

"What if I don't want to change anything?" She continued to go through the contract. Pointing at the places I needed to sign along the way.

"Then use the money to pay rent or something."

"I didn't know you could get something like that."

"Most people don't, but that's why you have me on your team."

After signing on the last spot, I gave her a hug.

"Thanks for believing in me."

"I'm doing more than that."

"What?"

"I'm going to invest in you as well."

"Invest?"

"I get a commission for making this transaction happen. So, I'm going to give it to you as an investment." She smiled as she put the package back together.

"Ebonee! Are you serious?!" I grabbed her arm and jumped up from my seat. Before she could say anything else, I had hugged her neck really tight.

"Okay, okay. Don't choke me to death."

"I'm sorry. I'm just…"

"I know. Told you to believe and claim it and you shall receive it."

"Having you on my team doesn't hurt either. I promise you, Ebb, you won't be disappointed."

CHAPTER 6

eCoys, Inc. was up and running and I have to admit, business had been good. We'd been operating off of word-of-mouth advertising alone.

Just as promised, Felicia had told not only the friend she'd mentioned, but a few others as well. It reminded me of that old shampoo commercial they used to play when I was a kid. She told a friend, who told a friend, and so on, and so on, and—well, you get the picture.

My cousin, LaNasha, and a few of her friends were on the payroll as decoys. With them doing the assignments, I was able to stay in the office and handle other important things.

Cara had been worth her weight in gold. As promised, she arrived early and left late. I made sure she was more than compensated for it, too.

"Deeva, we had a call come in from another potential client." Cara handed me the preliminary questionnaire form we used to screen callers.

"Did she say when she wanted to come in?" I looked over the sheet.

"She wants to come in Monday, but I'm not going to be in the office. You know, I have that appointment. You think you can take her?"

I tried to have as little contact with the clients as possible. Cara was the only face they could put to DeCoys for precautionary reasons.

I looked over the sheet again. It seemed harmless enough. I opened the planner I kept on my desk.

"I can take her around eleven. Make sure she gets here on time, because I have a lunch date at twelve-thirty." I penciled her name in.

"Did you run the rest of the checks on her?"

"Yeah. She checked out. No priors as a stalker."

"Okay. Make up a file for her and leave it on my desk. I'll look over it again Monday morning." I unplugged my PDA and earpiece that were charging.

"Where are you rushing off to? You got a hot date or something?"

"When's the last time I had a date?"

"I think it's time you have one then. You've been married to this business long enough. What you need to do is go out dancing." She rolled her hips from one side to the other.

"Then round up the girls and tell me where to meet ya'll and what time. I'll be there as soon as I finish up."

"You still haven't told me where you're going."

"And you think you'd get the hint."

"Okay. Be that way then. You know you're going to tell me later."

I smiled and walked out.

"We heard you went on some sort of secret booty call."

"Just goes to show you, you can't believe everything you *hear*." I shot Cara a playful, nasty look.

"Whatever. We're here to have a good time." Ebonee signaled for the waitress.

"Deeva, I think you have a fan lurking about." Cara nodded her head in the direction of the table where four guys were seated.

"Girl, please. They could be looking at any one of us. Why you gotta assume it's me?"

"I'm not talking about the whole table. I'm talking dude in the blue. The one with the beard. The tall, red one."

"You know how much she likes the red ones."

They all laughed at Lisa's attempt to add a little humor.

"You're a riot." I shifted in my seat and quickly glanced over at the table again.

Umm. He was cute.

"Deeva, did you hear me?"

"Cara, I'm not thinking about you."

"That's obvious. But, I was saying, why don't you go over and introduce yourself?"

"You're really cute."

"That's obvious, too."

"Here comes the waitress," Ebonee announced as if she were saying "*Thank God.*"

Appetizers and drinks were passed around.

"So, what's going on with everyone? It's been a while since we've all gotten together like this." I sipped my sweet tea.

"No, it's been a while since you've gotten together with all of us," Lisa said as she bopped her head to the beat.

"Hey, don't hate on Deeva 'cause she's doing her thing."

"Ebonee, you don't have to defend me." I glared at Lisa.

"I didn't mean it as a bad thing. I was just saying it has been a minute since she's been out in a public setting with us."

"Okay then. What's going on with you guys?" I looked at Lisa.

"Nothing you don't already know. It's not like Cara doesn't keep you informed of *everything*." Lisa continued to bounce to the beat.

"What's your problem tonight?"

"Nothing." She shrugged her shoulders.

I gave Cara a look, which told her to leave it alone. If anything else was said and she continued with her shitty attitude, I was bound to curse her out. I chalked it up to a potential bad day at work.

Before I could get my next thought together, the distinct sound of a man clearing his throat came from behind me.

"I hope I'm not intruding."

"Go right ahead and intrude," Ebonee replied.

He had the attention of all the ladies at the table.

"I see you ladies are having what I presume to be a

girl's night out, but I would kick myself if I didn't take advantage of this opportunity to come over and at least find out your name."

He leaned in to my ear.

Before I could respond, Cara had begun to run off all my information.

"Deeva McCoy. That's D-e-e-v-a."

"I can speak for myself."

His smile lit up his handsome face. He came around and stood on the side of me and reached out to shake my hand.

"Tristan Savage."

I looked at his hand—large with long fingers—that was awaiting mine.

"As you already know…" I shot Cara a look. "I'm Deeva McCoy. It's nice to meet you, Tristan Savage."

"Is it possible for us to talk? You know—"

"Well, since the food is all gone, I'm going to call it a night." Ebonee reached for her purse and pulled out some money to help cover the bill. Cara placed her money with Ebonee's.

"Why we got to leave? He came over here. If he really wants to talk to her he can take her to another table." Lisa rolled her eyes and looked away.

Almost embarrassed, I picked up the money everyone had put down and replaced it with my credit card. It wasn't lost on me that Lisa, who was acting like an über-bitch, was the only one who hadn't reached in her purse.

"I know you don't think this was on the house?" Evidently I wasn't the only one who had noticed. Ebonee gave Lisa a look, which more than said she needed to pay up.

"This wasn't my idea. Shit, I didn't really have anything but a glass of sweet tea." She reached in her purse and tossed a five-dollar bill on the table.

I took a deep breath.

Cara threw the bill back at her. "Sweet tea, my ass. You ate just like the rest of us."

"Look, I don't feel like this becoming a scene." I passed the card and the bill to the waitress.

"What the hell is your problem, Lisa?" Ebonee asked through clenched teeth.

"Why do I have to be the one with a problem?"

"Something's got to be wrong with you. I mean, you've been snippy all night."

"No, I haven't."

I looked at Tristan. "I'm really sorry about this."

Ebonee and Cara had gotten up and were gathering their things.

"Lisa, why are you waiting? It's not like you're expecting change. Let's go." Ebonee placed her purse on the table in front of her.

Lisa shot me a look and then slowly got up.

"We don't usually act this way. So, don't hold it against Deeva," Cara added before she kissed me on the cheek.

"I'll see you at the office in the morning."

Lisa grabbed her jacket and purse. "Ya'll are always

trying to accuse me of something. I work hard every day. It's not like covering my part is going to break you. Shit, I remember having to do it for ya'll a few times."

"Look, I got you. It's cool." I signed the bill.

"I'm sorry, Deeva, maybe I should—"

"No. It's fine. Now is as good a time as any for us to talk." I gave him my most convincing smile. It must have worked since he took a seat across the table from me. I casually scanned the room before settling my gaze back on him.

"You know first meetings can be really awkward sometimes?"

He laughed. His smile complemented his handsome face.

"They sure can be. Don't feel bad. I know how friends can stress you out. I have a few I'd like to tell where to get off, but they'll still be my boys at the end of the day."

My smile hid my true thoughts. I wanted to do more than tell Lisa where to get off. What I really wanted to do was slap her ass silly, in the hopes of rattling her brain back into working order. I wasn't going to think about that right then. My focus was going to be on the good-looking man seated in front of me.

"So, Mr. Savage, tell me more about you?"

"I like a woman who asks for exactly what she wants."

I laughed a bit.

"In my line of work, I find it's easier to get all the formalities out of the way."

"Then why don't we do this." He looked down at his

watch. "It's getting late and, as much as I would love to sit and talk to you all night, we both have to get up early in the morning, Besides, I'd like to have more time, so I can answer any questions you may have. With that said, why don't we exchange numbers? I'll give you a call to make sure you got home safely tonight and then I'll ask you out for a date. Tomorrow night. Hopefully you'll say yes, and we'll get the *formalities* out of the way then."

I waited for a moment before I said anything. Bit gently on the corner of my bottom lip as I pretended to be giving his suggestion some serious thought. I then reached for my purse and searched through it for a pen and something to write on.

"Here." I slid my number across to him. He placed his hand on mine and looked at me. I could feel a warmth building at the spot where the end of his fingers sat. I pulled my hand from beneath his and passed him the pen. He wrote his information on the other half of the paper I'd used.

"Now, you promise to call me when you get home?" He held the paper out to me between his two fingers.

"I thought you were going to call me."

"I think it would work out better if you called me, once you got home. Since I don't know how long it's going to take you to get there. I wouldn't want to seem like a stalker if you got home and saw my number on your caller ID five times."

"A man with a great sense of humor—I like that."

"So, do you promise to call me once you get home?"

"I promise."

"Cool." I took the number from him and placed it in my purse next to my cell.

I waited ten minutes after I got in to call and then talked to him until a little after two.

spent the better part of the day getting myself prepared for my dinner date later that evening. Hair appointment. Nails and feet were done. I even stopped by the MAC counter to get my makeup professionally done.

It had been a while since I'd been on a first date and I wanted to look my best. Hopefully he was taking me somewhere worthy of all my hard work.

I checked myself in the mirror one last time before turning off the light. I walked into the kitchen and checked the clock on the microwave.

He should be here in fifteen minutes.

I checked my cell phone to see if he had called while I was in the bathroom earlier. No missed calls had registered on the incoming call list. A good sign he hadn't decided to back out.

The minutes seemed to creep by. The closer it got to seven and he hadn't arrived yet, the more I began to think he had decided to stand me up. At 6:57 my doorbell rang. After looking through the peephole, I placed my hand on the doorknob and took a deep breath before opening the door.

He was dressed in an all-black ensemble. Black jacket. Black slacks. Black button-down shirt. It was a definite complement to the simple black dress I had chosen to wear.

"Sorry I'm late. I had to make a quick stop by my mom's." He handed a bouquet of flowers to me. "I thought you'd like these."

The gesture was enormous. I hadn't gotten flowers from a man since my high school graduation. And those were from my daddy.

"Thank you so much. Let me put them in some water before we leave." I walked back into the kitchen.

"You can have a seat," I called over my shoulder.

I grabbed the Pillar Vase Ebonee had given me as a housewarming gift from the cabinet and filled it with water.

"Did you have a hard time finding me?"

"No. I have a GPS system. You're actually not that far from me. I'm about twenty minutes east of here. Out in Stone Mountain."

"Stone Mountain? My girlfriend Lisa lives out there." I dried my hands and walked back to join him in the living room.

He was looking at the various pictures I had on the walls and shelves throughout the room.

"I like these black frames."

"Thanks. Ebonee loves to decorate. She pretty much helped me with the whole house."

I grabbed my purse and jacket from the arm of the chair. He walked over to where I was standing.

"You have a really nice place."

"Thank you. Ready?"

We pulled up to the valet stand and waited our turn. One attendant opened my door while another ran around the car to open his.

"Welcome to Emeril's. I hope you enjoy your dining experience with us tonight."

I smiled and thanked him while Tristan got the valet ticket from the other guy. As soon as we began to walk toward the door of the restaurant, the sound of screeching tires caused Tristan to turn around and look. All he could see was the red of his taillights as the attendant sped into the parking garage across the way. He shook his head.

"Sometimes I prefer to park my own car."

We continued into the restaurant. Tristan checked in with the hostess while I waited off to the side.

"Reservation for Savage."

"Good evening, Mr. Savage. Your table will be ready shortly."

I was more than impressed with his choice. Especially once we were seated in the dining area inside the huge rocket-shaped, wine tower.

"Since I didn't know exactly what you like to eat, I thought this would be a safe choice."

"This was a very good choice. Your cool-points score went way up with this one." I gave him a pleasing smile and a wink.

Conversation flowed as we enjoyed the top-notch service and enticing food. We went through the motions of a first official date—getting-to-know-you questions were asked and answered.

I learned quite a few things about Tristan Savage.

He'd never been married. Has one child—a ten-year-old son that he had sole custody of. His son's mother had been his high school sweetheart. She had gotten caught up in the wrong element two years after their son was born and ended up hooked on drugs. He did all he could to help her, but to no avail. The streets had a stronger pull on her than he or their child, so she would always end up back on them chasing her next high.

"I worked hard to provide a decent life for us. She didn't have to do anything but go to school." There was a hint of sadness that settled behind his eyes.

"I put off going to college once she got pregnant. While going to college had been a dream of mine, I don't regret the decision I made. The happiest day of my life was the day my son was born." His smile started to come back as the memory registered.

"So, where is she now?" I pushed my plate away with the small piece of bread pudding on it.

"She overdosed two years ago."

I took a large gulp of water and coughed a bit. His answer had totally caught me off guard.

"I was expecting it. She was really out there by then. She was nothing more than a shell of herself the last time she came by the house looking for me to sponsor a high. My son didn't deserve that."

I stretched my eyes and took a deep breath as I searched for something to say.

"What about you, Deeva? Any children? Ever been married? Who is Deeva McCoy?"

I knew he was attempting to lighten the mood.

"Let's see. I've never been married. Ah, I don't have any children. At least, not yet." I thought about how I would be able to tell him I had my own business without getting into exactly what it was that I did. My stock answer was I worked at an advertising firm.

Earlier he told me he had been at MARTA for fifteen years. He'd been employed there from the age of eighteen.

"Are you originally from Atlanta? Or are you like most people around here? A transplant from somewhere else."

"Yes, I'm a transplant. I've been here for a long time, though. Went to college and decided to stay."

"That's understandable. Seeing how most people who're not from here arrived here via the AUC. Where are you originally from?"

"I was born in Northern Virginia, but my parents

moved us to Daytona Beach when I was in kindergarten."

"Don't you miss the water? Both of those places have some of the most beautiful beaches."

"I prefer to swim in the pool over the beach. Going to the beach was never really one of my favorite outings."

He smiled.

"I take it the answer is no, then."

"Are *you* originally from here?"

"A Grady baby," he said with pride. "So was my mother, my father, all my siblings, and my son."

"A native Atlantian. You're almost a rarity. Like looking for dinosaurs," I joked.

"I don't know now. There are quite a few of us who were born and raised here who still live here. Sometimes I don't understand why so many people come here and fall in love with the place."

"Uh, the cost of living is cheaper. You can actually afford to buy a really nice home in a pleasant area without giving up essentials like food. And the most important thing of all, there are plenty of black folks doing positive things here." I ticked each one off on my fingers.

"Need I say more?"

"No. I get the picture."

"Are you saying you don't have hometown pride?"

"Oh, I have plenty of hometown pride."

"Okay."

We had spent more than an ample amount of time in the restaurant before finally leaving. He held my hand as we walked out to get the car.

"If I haven't told you before, you look really beautiful tonight."

I knew my cheeks were turning a shade of crimson.

Tristan handed the valet his ticket for the car.

"Yo, my man. Take it easy this time," he said to the attendant.

The guy shook his head in agreement before darting off to get the car.

"I know my ride isn't a Benz, BMW, or…" He tilted his head toward the line of expensive cars sitting in front of the restaurant.

"Hey, a Maxima is a nice car."

"And it's new."

"I hear ya." I slapped his hand in agreement. We both laughed.

The valet pulled up and ran around to open the door for me.

"Thank you," I said as I slid into the soft, black leather seat.

"Where to now?" Tristan asked as he closed his door.

I shrugged my shoulders

"Are you ready to call it a night?"

"If you're tired of me—"

"See, why did you have to go there?" I smiled.

"I was asking because I was thinking we could head over to this other spot."

I glanced at my watch. It was close to ten.

"That sounds good."

"I don't know if you've ever been to this place, but

they have a really nice set on Saturday nights." He pulled off from the valet stand.

My cell phone began to vibrate. I searched in my bag for it. The screen showed Ebonee's smiling face. I had a feeling she was going to call to see how my date was going. I was tempted to hit the IGNORE button, but thought better of it.

"Yes, Ebb?"

"What? Slow down, Ebonee, I can't understand what you're saying."

Her breathing sounded labored.

"Are you home?" I was starting to worry. It had been a while since she'd had an asthma attack.

"I'm on my way." I hung up the phone and looked at Tristan. "She's having an asthma attack!"

"Put her address in," he commanded. Concern was on his face as I fumbled around with the buttons on his GPS system. He grabbed my hand to steady it and asked me to repeat her address to him. He hit the buttons on his GPS system and we were on our way.

CHAPTER 8

We pulled into Ebonee's community about twenty minutes later. Stately homes lined the street. Each one with no less than three-car garages, all sitting on at least an acre. We continued down the tree-lined street until we reached her house and pulled into the circular driveway near the front door. I was out the car before Tristan had stopped the car.

"Ebonee," I called out as I ran up the steps to her porch. I pressed on the doorbell a few times before knocking. "Ebonee, open the door!" My panicky knock turned into a desperate bang.

I fished around in my bag for my keys. I had a key for "just in case" instances—like these.

I began to fear the worst when she hadn't gotten to the door. My hands began to tremble causing me to drop my bag. The contents around my feet, I continued to search for my keys until I suddenly heard them jingling. Tristan had retrieved them from the step behind me.

"Which one is it?" he asked.

I frantically searched the ring for the right key. Any

other time I would know it was the second key over from my office key. In the frazzled state I was in, I couldn't tell which key was which. He handed me back my bag, after placing everything that fell out back in it. Tristan walked over to the lock and then looked at the keys on my ring. The first key he tried clicked the lock open. At that moment, he had morphed into my knight-in shining-armor. I threw my arms around his neck before rushing into the house.

"Ebonee," I called out again. There were three floors to search.

"Tristan, the kitchen and family room are through there." I pointed to my left. "I'll check her bedroom." I ran in the opposite direction.

A million scenarios raced through my mind as I ran from her bedroom, her bathroom, and into her walk-in closet. No Ebonee. I feared I would find her sprawled out on the floor.

I rushed out the room and ran smack into Tristan. He grabbed me by my arm to keep me from losing my balance.

"She's not in there either?"

He shook his head.

"Do you think she's downstairs?"

I walked over to the railing of the first floor and looked down into what was traditionally a basement in any other house, but was a beautiful, open floorplan in this one. I called her name as Tristan ran down the stairs.

"I'm up here," I heard.

I sprinted up the stairs.

"Where are you?"

"I'm in here," came from the media room.

I ran down the hall and found her hemmed up in a corner with a broom in her hand.

"What the hell?"

Her face was streaked with black from where her tears and mascara had run together.

"Is someone in here?" I scanned the room and found nothing.

"Girl, what's wrong with you?" I walked closer to her. I could tell her breathing was a little shallow, which meant we needed to get her inhaler and quick.

"It's over there," she said in a low voice as she pointed to the other side of the room where the sofa was.

I looked, but didn't see anything.

"What's over there?"

Before she could respond, a small animal ran from under the wall unit, straight underneath the sofa.

"What the hell?" I ran over to where Ebonee was.

"He was in the attic and when I…" She paused to take a breath. "I opened the door…" She stopped to breathe again.

"Okay. Okay. Where's your inhaler?"

She pointed down. "In my purse."

"Tristan!" I yelled. "Come upstairs! Hurry! Please!"

I could hear his heavy footsteps as he hastily mounted

the stairs. I guess the squirrel heard him also, because he ran from underneath the sofa and jumped up on the table near the window, looking for a way out.

"Tristan—"

He ran into the room and surveyed the situation. I could see a grin forming on his face.

"It's not funny." I laughed a bit myself.

Ebonee's breathing seemed to get a bit more labored. The situation that seemed to be humorous a moment ago could quickly turn into a grave one, if we didn't get her inhaler to her.

Tristan looked around, searching for something to help him get the squirrel out of the room.

"I have to get her inhaler." I grabbed Ebonee's clammy hand.

"You guys come on, while I block him."

The squirrel scurried into the other corner. I took the opportunity and made a move to leave the room. Ebonee was with me, but stopped and clutched her chest.

Tristan ran over to Ebonee.

"Go and get her inhaler," he ordered as he knelt down and scooped Ebonee up.

I rushed down the stairs and into Ebonee's room and found her purse on her dresser. I dumped the contents out and searched through her things, but found no inhaler.

Tristan carried Ebonee into the room and placed her on the bed.

"Ebonee, I don't see it," I said frantically.

She began to shake her head.

"What?" I was beginning to get anxious as I watched her struggle to breathe.

She pointed to the chaise lounge near the window where another purse sat. I ran over and grabbed it.

"You need to stick to one damn purse," I chided as I dug inside the purse until I felt the plastic of the inhaler. I tossed it to her and watched as she took two long puffs.

Tears were running down her face. She closed her eyes and waited for her breathing to even out. She continued to take a few more deep gasps. The minutes passed slowly as I watched her with bated breath—no pun intended.

"Whew," Ebonee said. She looked over at Tristan. "You're my hero."

"What about me?" I asked sarcastically.

"Girl, did you not see this man pick my big ass up from the floor like I weighed a mere hundred pounds? He then proceeded to run down the stairs carrying me. You know I appreciate you and all, but if this doesn't work out…" She fanned her pointer finger back and forth between me and Tristan. "Look a sistah up."

"I'm glad to see your sense of humor is still intact. You scare me damn near half to death, had me running around this big-ass house, and he gets all the thanks. Friends! See if I come next time the squirrel makes an appearance."

She looked toward the ceiling, then over to Tristan. In all the excitement of getting her breathing under control, she'd almost forgotten what had started the whole thing.

Tristan winked and got up. "I got it."

CHAPTER 9

"What a way to end a first date." I looked at Tristan. He pulled into my driveway.

"It's definitely one for the memory books." He smiled as he put his car in park and cut the engine.

"Seems like everything is turning out to be one for the memory books between us." I laughed as I thought about the scene from the night before, when we met.

We sat silently. An awkward teenage moment hovered in the air. You know, the kind where you wonder what's going to happen next as your brain goes on hiatus, causing you to become a deaf mute momentarily. I decided to break the moment before it lingered too long and messed up the nice groove we'd created all the way there.

"Sorry we didn't get a chance to go to the place you were talking about earlier. Maybe we can take a rain check."

"Hey, she needed us. I'm glad we got there when we did. No telling what would've happened if we hadn't."

"Yeah. It doesn't happen that often, but her asthma—"

"My brother had it really bad when we were kids. One

time, he almost died. Had to be rushed to the hospital. Mama thought his lungs had collapsed." He seemed to have a faraway look in his eyes as he remembered.

"I don't know what we would've done had you not been there." I thought about how he had stepped in and taken control of the situation. I was turned on then, and was beginning to be turned on again, just thinking about it. I took a deep breath and opened the car door. Tristan, eyes wide open at the sudden movement, jumped out the car and rushed from his side so he could hold the door open for me.

This man.

I smiled at him as he waited for me to exit the car. We walked the short distance to my front door. I turned around to face him.

"I had a really good time tonight. I mean, up until the episode at Ebonee's house."

"It wasn't as bad as you think." He laughed. He slipped his hands in his pockets.

I battled between asking him to come inside, or sending him on his merry way. The good girl-bad girl battle was going on something fierce inside my head. Seeing how he was still standing there, the bad girl won out. I unlocked the door and stood to the side so he could enter.

"Would you like something to drink? Water; soda; a glass of wine?" I called out as I made my way through the living room and into the kitchen. I placed my purse on the counter.

"You make the choice." He sat at the breakfast bar and watched as I moved around the kitchen in search of wine glasses.

I know what other choice I want to make. The bad girl was hard at work, filling my head with ideas. As I poured the wine, I thought about what Ebonee had said as I was leaving out the door. "Girl, you better get you some of that sexy-ass man tonight. Put away all those silly rules you like to live by and be adventurous."

"You want me to sleep with him on the first date?"

"Stop being a prude. Women are doing it more now than ever. Men don't give a damn if it's the first date or the *twenty-first* date. As long they're getting sex, they're happy."

I shook my head, then hugged her.

"I thought you were working on changing. Maybe you took too many hits off your inhaler. I'll call and check on you tomorrow."

"Don't call me unless—"

"Good night, Ebonee."

Her words were ringing loudly as I thought about how it would feel to be in his arms; to have his lips on my most sensual parts. Wondered what kind of lover he was.

"Here you go." I handed him the glass of wine. "I like wines that are on the sweet side. I hope that doesn't bother you."

"You could've given me a glass of Boones Farm and I would've been okay."

I couldn't help but laugh. I think Boones Farm had

been an introductory wine for most young people, who didn't have parents who drank other wine at home.

I walked around to where he was seated at the breakfast bar. As I was going to sit on the barstool next to his, my inner bad girl suddenly reared her head. Before I could chicken out and change my mind, I stood in front of him and placed my glass on the counter to his side. Slowly, I placed a kiss on his luscious lips. His response was favorable as he pulled me closer. I could've stayed that way forever, but the bad girl was at it again. His hand in mine, I led him upstairs to my bedroom.

"You sure you want to do this?"

I placed a finger over his lips to quiet him.

He didn't say another word until we were both undressed. A tangled mass of limbs. Our heat and passion filled the atmosphere as we discovered each other's bodies. He kissed the soft places of my waist—loving every inch of my full figure. I returned the gesture; licking and sucking his nipples, which seemed to drive him crazy. After our intense session of foreplay, we were ready to move forward to the main event. He prepared himself with a condom. Parted my legs with his knees. As he entered me, he stared into my eyes, watching my facial expressions. The rush of blood throughout my body almost sent me over the edge. He began an even, slow stroke. I rode each and every wave until we both crashed against the shore of ecstasy—me reaching mine before him.

Panting and wet from sweat, he rolled off of me. It took

a few moments for me to catch my breath. My heart rammed against my breastbone. He got up and went into the bathroom. I could hear the faucet running. All kind of thoughts began to run through my head—none of them good at that point.

I knew it wasn't a good idea. No man wants a woman who's willing to have sex with him on the first date. *What does Ebonee know? I'll lay here and pretend I'm out of it so he can make a clean getaway.*

A few moments later, he emerged. My head was facing the opposite way, so I didn't have to watch him leave. Suddenly, I felt the bed shift from his weight as he climbed back into the bed. I turned to look at him.

"Open your legs," he said softly.

He smiled as I gave him a look, which asked what the hell was going on.

He held up a washcloth.

"A warm rag." He took the towel and ever so gently began to wipe between my legs. Cleaning all traces left behind from my sexual eruption. That simple gesture made me melt like putty in his hands.

"Isn't that better?"

"Umm-hmm," was all I could get out.

Satisfied with the response, he smiled.

He placed the rag on the nightstand next to the bed and snuggled with me. It had been quite a while since I'd spooned with a man. His arms were wrapped protectively around me. A beautiful ending to a beautiful night.

Ebonee was going to get an earful the next day.

CHAPTER 10

After spending the weekend acting like a love-struck teen, it was Monday morning and time to get back to the grind.

My cell was ringing as soon as it powered up good.

"I haven't heard from you all weekend, so I know what you were up to."

I couldn't have stopped the smile from spreading across my face if I had vise grips.

Tristan had made me breakfast in bed twice. Yes, *twice*. And not simple fried eggs and juice either. There were omelets, filled with tomatoes, onions, cheese, and bacon. Then, on the side, were a few strips of turkey bacon, delicious buttered grits, toast, and freshly squeezed orange juice.

We'd enjoyed an outing at Piedmont Park, where we walked along the trail and enjoyed the sights. Then, later on that evening, we'd enjoyed a simple meal at Chipotle. This was all done on Saturday. On Sunday, we'd ended up down by the CNN Center, where we took in a free concert in Centennial Park thrown by a non-profit group called Hands On Atlanta.

Ebonee squealed with delight as I ran through the events of my weekend.

"I told you that man wasn't nothing but the truth. I'm so happy for you. So, when are you going out again?"

"Damn, Ebonee, he left my house this morning. I don't want to—"

"Whatever. This is the first man you've had since…" She paused. "Well, you know since what and who."

Yeah, I knew who she was talking about. But everyone knew the rules about him; his name was like the character Voldemort, from the Harry Potter books—one that was not to be spoken out loud. At least, not around me.

I opened my planner and scanned over my day. I had a few appointments so I needed to get going.

"Well, I'll give you a call once I get into the office. I'm already running late." I grabbed my bag from the dresser and headed for the front door.

"Don't forget."

"I won't, Ebb. Bye." I closed the phone and looked around to make sure I had turned off everything.

I arrived at the first stop of my morning, Starbucks. Mary, the barista, smiled at me as she passed me my morning ritual—a tall, white chocolate mocha with a blueberry scone.

"You're running a bit behind today. Long weekend?"

"Something like that." I grinned.

"Maybe you should get a grande instead," she suggested, pointing to the stack of larger-sized cups.

"No, I'm good." I swiped my card and said good-bye.

While I was a bit later than usual, I still arrived before the normal hours of business. Cara was already up and running when I walked in. She looked at me and shook her head with a grin on her face.

"Don't say a word." I placed my briefcase on my desk and took another sip of my coffee.

"I wasn't going to say anything. I see you still made it to get your liquid nicotine."

"Just because your ass is naturally peppy in the morning, don't hate on those of us who need a little help." I held my cup up to her as a toast.

"I keep telling you, tea is better for you. You don't have to worry about your breath stinking or your teeth being all stained up either. Plus, it comes in a variety of flavors."

"So does coffee."

"This is an argument for another day."

"Your schedule is on your desk. You have that appointment at eleven, the one we talked about on Friday."

"Yeah, I remembered. What time are you going to be back?" I pulled the folder from the stack on my desk and looked over the new notes she'd made.

"I wasn't sure how long it was going to take, so I cleared my schedule for the rest of the day."

"That's fine. I was actually going to suggest it to you."

"Did you get a chance to get any pictures of the mark yet?" I tapped the folder in my hand.

"Since this was a rush, I didn't, but I told her to bring

one with her." She passed me another folder from the stack on her lap.

"So are we going to talk about what you did this weekend?" She looked up at me with a sly grin on her face.

"There's not much to tell."

"Umm-hmm."

"Well, not *that* much to tell."

"Have you checked your messages at all this weekend?"

I'd scanned over the caller ID and I knew she'd called at least twice on Saturday and once on Sunday.

"I didn't have time to get around to checking it this weekend."

"Umm-hmm."

"Don't you have somewhere you have to be this morning?"

Our morning routine of going over new and closed cases was almost done. She took another sip of her herbal tea before placing the cup on the edge of my desk.

"Well, if we're finished here, I'm going to head on out. I'll give you a call and let you know how everything goes."

"Make sure you do." I got up to give her a hug. I knew her mind was probably working overtime with worry.

The alarm on my PDA and computer both went off, letting me know my next appointment was scheduled to arrive within the hour.

She looked at me before walking out the door. "After I give you my information about the test, I'll be expecting you to give me a full report of your weekend."

Once Cara left, I went back to work. Pulled the file from the small remaining stack on my desk and went over it again. I liked to familiarize myself with a case as much as possible before I met with a client.

Octavia Towers was prompt. At eleven sharp she was seated on the sofa across from me. I had my pad and pen ready to jot down any notes I thought would be helpful.

"How long have you been involved with this man?"

"Not too long."

"What's not too long?" I continued to jot down notes.

"Two months. Almost two months." She twisted the piece of napkin she had in her hand.

"Two months?"

"I know it doesn't seem like a long time by normal standards, but I'm thinking—or rather hoping—this relationship will be going to another level soon. Before I waste any more time than I already have, I need to know if it's worth it." She crossed and uncrossed her legs.

"I fully understand and that's the reason we offer these services. Here are a few things I'm going to need from you, in order to move forward." I handed her a list.

She carefully looked it over and pulled an envelope from her purse.

"My friend who recommended you told me to come prepared." She smiled coyly. "Here is a copy of his work schedule, personal schedule, a recent photo of him, and a photo of his car." She handed the envelope over to me.

I picked up my PDA and pulled up a schedule I kept for LaNasha and the other girls. I couldn't believe they'd all taken off the same weekend. Then I remembered them telling me something about some national convention for exotic dancers. I guess if they could have a pimp and players ball, the strippers/exotic dancers deserved one, too.

"Ms. Towers, the first available opening I have to get someone on this will be late next week."

"No! I need you to get on it this week!" She calmed down a bit, after seeing the expression on my face. "I'm sorry. It's just that I'm going to be out of town next week and, to be honest, the sooner you get on this for me, the better."

"I understand, but the girls I use—"

"Why can't you do it?"

I was shocked by her request. I smirked and shook my head.

"I try to stay away from that part of the business."

"So, you're telling me you're running a business you don't participate in fully?"

"No, that's not what I'm saying. What I'm saying is—"

"Then you'll do it? I mean, you're definitely a beautiful woman. What man wouldn't be tempted by you? You probably have men drooling over you." She pulled another envelope from her purse and handed it over to me. "I'm willing to pay extra if it will get it done sooner."

I fanned the envelope for a minute as I thought about what I was going to do. It had been a while since I'd actually gone out as a decoy. I pulled open the envelope enough to see the numbers on the cashier's check inside. I checked my schedule on my desk as I continued to think.

"You've certainly made it enticing."

"So, I should be expecting a report by the end of the week?" She got up. Her bag hung from the bend in her left elbow as her keys dangled from her index finger. She reached out to shake my hand.

I looked at the check again before rising to shake her hand.

"I'll give you a call either Friday or Monday."

"I'll be looking forward to it."

"Oh, by the way. What's his name?" I looked through the papers I had in my file.

"Tristan. Tristan Savage."

CHAPTER 11

I sat with the contents of the envelope she'd given me spread out on my desk. I tried to convince myself there was no possible way this could be the same guy. If the name hadn't been convincing, the smiling face in the picture in front of me was proof enough.

What were the odds? Not just the odds of me meeting him and sleeping with him on the first date after not dating for more than six months, but the odds of a woman coming to my office and talking me into being the one who's on the case.

I couldn't think of what to do. I felt as if he'd used me up all weekend only to run back to his girlfriend.

"How could I have been so stupid?" I placed my head on my arms on top of my desk.

While the visions of everything we'd done over the weekend flooded my mind, the feelings of how he made me feel flooded the lower parts of me. I could feel every kiss. Every touch. My cell started ringing. I took a deep breath and picked up the phone.

"Hello?"

"You know I've been waiting for you? I thought we were having lunch. Where are you?"

"Ebonee, can you meet me at my house?"

"What's wrong?"

"I'll tell you when you get there." I ended the call without another word.

"Wait a minute. Say that again. His *what* showed up at your office?"

"She said she was his *girlfriend*. A woman claiming to be in a relationship with him showed up at my office this morning. We both know when a woman comes to my office, she's there for one kind of service."

"To see if her man will cheat on her."

"Exactly."

"Have you talked to him today?"

"He told me he's on his route until three. He's supposed to call me when he gets off."

Ebonee looked at her watch.

"If he's true to his word, you should be hearing from him in about an hour."

"What am I supposed to say to him? Hey, I met your girlfriend this morning, but I can't exactly tell you how I found out she's your girlfriend."

"Now, Deeva McCoy, we all know you have more savvy about you than that. You're good at what you do. This is why you have a successful business."

"I know, but I never wanted to use my own services."

"Why not? You're a woman who's attracted to a man who just may be in a relationship with another woman. You make a living off of finding out this type of information. It doesn't make you stupid because you need your own services. It makes you smart enough to be able to do it without having to pay for it." She patted my leg and got up. She grabbed the dishes we'd used and took them into the kitchen.

"I feel so stupid, Ebonee. I mean, I haven't had this much fun with a man in a very long time. I've been trying to play it safe for years. The one time I let my guard down, and I mean *waaayy* down, this is what happens." I put my head against the back of the sofa.

Ebonee walked back in with my cell in her hand.

"It's ringing." She gave me a tightlipped smile as she passed it to me.

I looked at the name of the caller. With my eyes closed, I took a deep breath before saying, "Hello?"

"Hey, beautiful. I had to make a quick stop and couldn't resist calling you. How's your day been so far?"

"It's been interesting, to say the least."

"Interesting? How about I meet you at your house later? I'll stop off at the grocery store and get a few things, so I can make you a dinner you won't forget. Then you can tell me what was so fascinating about your day."

I was quiet for a moment. I wanted to get to the bottom of things and being at my place would give me a home-court advantage.

"Are you still there?"

"Sure."

"Sure you're still there or—"

"Sure, I'll see you when you get here."

"Okay. Good. Don't worry about anything. I'll bring everything we're going to need. Well, except for the dishes and pots I'm going to need to cook." He chuckled.

"Let me get off the phone. Ebonee is here and I'm being a bit rude."

"Oh. Okay. Tell her I said hello and I'll see you later."

"Bye."

Ebonee waited as I stared at the phone for a few seconds before placing it on the table in front of me.

"How did he sound?"

"There was a hint of excitement in his voice."

"Well, that's a good thing. Look, give him the benefit of the doubt before you persecute him. It wouldn't be the first time you've had a woman come in claiming to be in a relationship with the man, only to find out she's not being completely truthful with you about the dynamics of their relationship."

"I know, Ebonee, but I have to give the client the benefit of the doubt as well. This woman has paid quite a bit of money to get this information." I thought about the extra check she had included with her payment.

"I'm not saying she's not telling the truth, but there's still a possibility."

"I'll keep that in mind tonight."

"You need to also keep in mind that Tristan is a good guy."

"How did you come to that verdict after only meeting him twice?"

"I may have been wrong about Willie, but my track record has been on point ever since."

"Yes, you have, but there's always room for error."

"One question then."

"What?"

"Did he seem like he had someone waiting at home for him when he was with you this weekend?"

It was something to think about.

CHAPTER 12

At six sharp Tristan was at my door, his arms loaded down with paper bags from Publix. After placing the bags on the counter in the kitchen, he spun me around and gave me a juicy kiss on the lips.

"Umm, I've been thinking about doing that all day." He hugged me tightly. I halfheartedly returned the gesture.

He seemed to be animated this evening. Talking as I sat and watched him prepare us a meal. My mouth watered, watching him chop up the ingredients.

"What's this for?" I pointed to the shrimp and crab meat that had been set aside with chopped mango, a few slices of an orange and a lime, and a little chopped cilantro.

"That's for the Seafood Margarita." He pointed to the two huge margarita glasses he'd gotten down from my cabinet. "You're going to love it." He winked at me.

"What's this other stuff for, if we're having seafood?"

He smiled and continued to season the Cornish hens.

"The margaritas are the appetizers, and this is the main course. Cornish hens with an amaretto stuffing."

My mouth began to water from thinking about it. I took a sip of my Lambrusco.

"Do you need help with anything? I'm pretty good in the kitchen myself."

"You can burn?"

"Can't you tell by the spread of my hips?" I turned to the side so he could get a glimpse.

"You're not that big, Deeva. You're actually the size of a *real woman*."

"You know, I read that somewhere. Real women wear at least a size twelve or fourteen. I'm a comfortable twelve. A ten when I want to show off my curves."

"But you're what? Five-seven? Five-eight?"

"Five-seven."

"Your weight is well-proportioned. Thick in all the right places." He patted me on my butt as he passed by me to get an ingredient that he needed.

An hour later we were seated at the dining room table, holding hands as we blessed the delicious dinner he had prepared.

"Amen. Let's eat," he said as he clapped his hands and rubbed them together really fast.

I picked up my glass and took another sip of what was my second glass of wine for the evening.

"You know, Tristan. Things between us happened so fast, this past weekend. I'm starting to feel like maybe we didn't get a chance to cover some things I feel are important."

"Like what? I thought we pretty much covered everything over the weekend." He put a forkful of food in his mouth.

I picked up my fork and knife and began to cut up my meat. I continued to talk without looking at him.

"Well, one important thing I don't think we really covered was whether or not you were in a relationship prior to Friday night?" I placed the tiny piece of meat on the tip of my fork in my mouth. It was so delicious, I was tempted to postpone this talk until I was completely finished devouring my meal.

"You're supposed to eat the margarita first." He pointed to the glass in front of me.

"Oh, I'm sorry. This just looked so good." I brought the appetizer closer to me.

At that point, we were both quiet. I tried to avert my eyes when I caught him looking at me.

"Can I ask you a question?" He continued to chew as he waited for my response.

I nodded and took another sip of my wine. The food was so delicious, I was seriously regretting my timing for starting the conversation.

"Where is this line of questioning coming from? After the weekend we spent together, do you really think I would put all this time and energy into starting something new, when I have someone already?"

I continued to enjoy the mouthful of food before I responded.

"In my time, I've seen some men who would do that and then some. Not to say you're that type of man. I just want to be careful. I can really see this being something special and I need to know if you have someone else."

"Right now, I'm not in a serious relationship with anyone. Do I date? Yes, I've gone on a few dates, but nothing serious."

"Are you searching for something serious? Or better yet, do any of these women you…" I pumped my fingers in the air. "…date think it's something serious?"

"In my defense—"

"Oh, here we go."

"Hear me out now. It's not like I'm going out with a different woman every night. I've been out with two different women in the past few months."

I waited for him to continue.

"So, I'm not some player out here running wild in the streets, talking about sowing my wild oats."

"Have you gone out more than twice with them?"

"Only one of them, but only because we have mutual friends. Now that I think about it, we've only gone on an actual date once. All the other times we've been together have been in group settings." He looked as if he was thinking about something, then shook his head and continued to eat.

"What was that about?"

He looked at me.

"I just thought about her."

"Her who?"

"You're pretty brutal tonight."

"I don't want to start things off with lies. I really enjoyed this past weekend and this meal." I pointed to the spread on the table with my fork. "This is the icing on the cake. I'm simply trying to make sure the cake I'm getting is a flavor I can stand to eat." I ate the last of my seafood margarita.

"I like how you said that. I respect your feelings and want to be straight up with you. Her name is Octavia."

My head jerked as I tried to hide the turmoil I was feeling inside.

"So, does she think the two of you are in a relationship? If she does, is there a good reason for thinking such a thing?" I was trying to get to the heart of the matter. I felt as if I had everything crossed; from my fingers down to my toes.

"If you're asking if we've been intimate…"

I cut him off. "I'm not trying to get *that* personal."

"Well, we haven't. It's just…" He paused for a moment. "She's not good with rejection."

"You're saying you've turned her down, but she doesn't get the picture."

"Not to mention her friend—who happens to be engaged to my friend—is always trying to put us in situations where we're coupled up together."

"What do you mean?" I continued to eat.

"Okay, for example, my friend and his girl have functions at their house all the time. One, in particular, is game night. Well, every time they choose teams, his girl is quick to put me and Octavia together."

"Are there any other single people there?"

"Yes."

I had to smile. The girls and I had been guilty of playing the hookup game; especially Ebonee. She'd wanted me to date one of Willie's lame-ass friends so we could double date. In our case, I was Tristan, but probably not as nice.

"So, what's her name is not hearing you when you say you're not interested?"

"Seems like none of them are hearing me. My boy. His girl. I think they're the ones fueling her pursuit to keep trying to make something out of nothing."

So, her girl is telling her things are about to go to the next level, but somewhere deep inside she must have a feeling of doubt. That's why she came to me.

"Have you told your friend to back off?"

"I told him *and* his girl, but she's one of those people who's convinced she knows what's best for everybody."

"Sounds to me like you're going to have to show them, by bringing someone else around. Or you're going to have to stop hanging with them altogether."

"Yo', seriously, I've been thinking about that. Maybe I can start hanging with you and your girls."

"I should let you know, sometimes we have more than our share of drama. You saw that the other night."

He chuckled.

"Have you talked to her yet? You know, your friend from the other night?" He went back to eating his food.

"I've been busy—with you." I looked at him and smiled.

"A good busy, right?"

"A very good busy."

He looked at my plate.

"Have we covered what needed to be covered?"

"Yes, we have. Thank you for your honesty. It's something that's hard to come by nowadays."

"I'll always be honest with you. I hope you offer me the same courtesy."

"I will."

"I'm serious now. You have to promise me we'll always be honest with one another. No matter how hard the truth may be. Promise?"

I looked at him for a second.

"I promise."

CHAPTER 13

"The man told you he's not interested in her." Ebonee was blasting off her knowledge of love in my ear through the phone. "Besides, you said yourself she didn't sound as if she was too sure about where the relationship was going, or if it was going at all."

Octavia had indeed suggested things between them were not solid.

"I don't know what to tell her. Hell, I don't know if I should be the one to tell her anything." I leaned my head against the headrest and closed my eyes.

"Let Cara handle her."

Leave it to Ebonee to think of something that would more than suffice.

"You know Cara; she'll tell her she needs to find someone else to focus on, and a few other things if needed."

That was one way to handle it, but I'd never been one to run from any type of confrontation.

"No, I think I should be the one to handle it."

"You don't have to always be in control, you know."

"I'm not trying to control—"

"Yes, you are. Look, Cara will handle talking to her. That's the usual protocol anyway. Cara handles the clients so you don't have to have too much contact with them. You've already broken protocol for her once. Let Cara handle it."

"We'll see."

"Deeva, you need to enjoy yourself for once. You have a successful business life, but your personal one sucks."

"Thank you, Dr. Love."

"As always, you're welcome."

"Well, let me get off this phone and get prepared for work."

"Did he spend the night last night?"

"You're so nosey." I knew she could hear the smile in my voice.

"Umm-hmm. He's working you overtime. Came and cooked you a dinner fit for a queen. Set the mood and went in for the attack."

"Girl, if you would have tasted that food."

"Shit, my clothes would've probably been off before I took the last bite. You know I have a special place in my heart for food, as it is. To have a man cook for me? And a gourmet meal at that?"

"Bye, crazy girl." I was laughing so hard I thought I was going to choke.

When I got into the office, Cara hadn't arrived yet. She'd called me the afternoon before to let me know her test had come back fine. It was a relief to all of us. Ever since she'd shared with us the doctor thought he saw something on her mammogram, we'd all been worried. She had a history of breast cancer in her family, which was the reason she'd gone in the first place.

She came in ten minutes later.

"So, what happened yesterday with your meeting?" she called out as she made her way into her office.

She had enough on her mind and I really didn't want to burden her with what was going on with me.

"I'll tell you all about it when you get in here." I finished off my cup of java and took the cup into the kitchen to dispose of it. When I returned to my office, Cara was seated and waiting.

"What happened?" She was going through a file on her lap.

"Girl, you know LaNasha and the rest are gone to their convention thing this week?"

"Yeah. I marked it on your calendars."

"Well, I tried to tell her I wouldn't be able to get anyone on it for another week. She didn't want to hear it. So, she proceeded to talk me into doing it."

"You agreed?"

"Yes, I agreed. She had a way with words, is all I'll say."

Cara laughed.

"She even sweetened up the pie. Added a nice lil' bonus and everything."

"Okay."

"She hands me the information in an envelope and then leaves."

Cara was starting to look confused.

I handed the envelope to her so she could see for herself. I watched as she read through the preliminary questionnaire we gave to all our clients. As soon as I saw her eyes buck open wide, I started to laugh.

"Are you *serious*?"

"I'll finish putting together her file, then I'll call her."

"Call her? You asked him about it?"

"I broached the subject last night when we were having dinner."

"And he said?"

I told her what Tristan had told me. How his friend and his girl were trying to hook them up.

"We've all been guilty of that. Hell, Ebonee was always trying to set somebody up with one of Willie's friends. Remember the one with the curly perm? Ugh!"

"Curly perm and gold teeth."

We cracked up laughing.

"So, it's definitely a credible story."

I nodded. "Ebonee thinks so, too."

"Well…" She got up and grabbed the file from my desk. "I'll give her a call either Friday or Monday, and let her know our findings."

"Look at this new file." Cara passed it over to me.

"They've been married for how long?"

"No, not that. Look at what LaNasha reported."

I ran my finger down the page to the typed report. My eyes went back and forth faster than a tennis match before abruptly stopping.

"A fucking man?! Are you serious?"

"I think we need to hire a few boys for the fam. Catch a few of these nasty-ass DL Negroes. It's bad enough a sistah has to deal with another woman, but another man? That's the lowest of lows."

"How did Nasha find out?"

"Girl, the dude was all up in his face before she could make a move. She said once she got a chance to talk to him, homeboy had an attitude and walked out. Here's the kicker; the mark left Nasha and ran out to follow him."

All I could do was shake my head.

"We might need to hire some guys for real."

"You trippin'. You need to *really* look into it. You know we can go to Lenox and recruit."

"Now you know you're wrong for that." I laughed.

It seemed to be a known fact that more than an ample amount of gay men in Atlanta frequented Lenox Mall.

"You are truly crazy."

"Crazy, hell. If you don't want to do it, I will. Ain't no shame in my game."

Although I was laughing, what she was saying made plenty of sense. It would be a way to expand our business. We all knew somebody whose man was suspect.

"Let's talk about it a little more before we make any decisions."

"You're the boss." She closed the file and went on to the next one.

"What's on the schedule for lunch today?"

"I was planning to get out of here early. I have a few errands I need to run before I head home." I was reading over a proposal for setting up a website for the company.

"Are you feeling okay?" Cara got up and placed her hand on my forehead. I slapped it away.

"I'm fine. Gosh, you've been telling me how you can handle things without me being in the office. Here's your chance to show me."

"Then get going." She got up and started to gather my things.

"I'm going in a minute."

"Let me take my stuff in my office. I'll see you later."

I finished off what I was working on, shut everything down or off. I stuck my head in Cara's office to say good-bye.

"See ya tomorrow." I waved.

"Tell Tristan I said hello," she called out behind me.

"I will."

CHAPTER 14

Leaning back against Tristan, I swept a handful of bubbles toward my chest.

"Is it hot enough?"

"Umm-hmm."

It had been a busy week in the office. Business had definitely picked up since we'd brought the boys on board. They were a lively bunch, to say the least. Gave us the information we wanted and then some at times. Lonnie was the leader. He would look at the pictures of the mark and tell us right off the bat if we needed to assign one of the girls or one of the boys. Cara and I were more than amused with him. So much so, we made a position that kept him in the office with us on most days.

"Okay, Girlfriend. I need you to not get things twisted. This one right here should be handled by Remy. Dude right here looks like he goes for the green-eyed, curly-haired ones."

"Lonnie, how do you know this? This man has two children with this woman."

"And?! You and I both know that don't have a damn thing to do with it. A booty bandit isn't worried about what's at home. The only thing on his mind is his thing and the one attached to the other body he's with."

"Okay now. You don't have to go into details about it."

"Women kill me, acting like they're not the least bit interested in what goes on when a man has sex with another man. That's why E. Lynn's books are flying off the shelves. And I don't think it's because of his gay following, okay." He snapped his fingers in the air as an added emphasis.

We couldn't do anything but giggle. I, myself, had pretty much every book E. Lynn Harris had written up until that point. The first two being a couple of my all-time favorites.

"I'll admit I was curious until I read *B-Boy Blues*. E. Lynn Harris is quite tame compared to James Earl Hardy. He is extremely visual," Cara added.

"Oh yes!" Lonnie's excitement meter climbed.

"He writes about the kinda brothas I love. Ain't nothing like a homie-lover-friend." He did a side jump, hip-hop move with a lil' Harlem Shake on the end of it.

"You talking about a homo thug? Walk around here acting all hard, but get them in the bedroom…"

"How would you know what they do when they get in the bedroom?"

"His ass is either getting fucked, or fucking another man. I think that sums it up."

"So, you're trying to say just because a man is gay, that he can't be hard?"

"Uh, duh," Neck craned forward a bit and eyes stretched, Cara intended to stand her ground.

Lonnie was about to really get into her ass behind this one.

"See, that's what's wrong with women today. They have this misperception that if a man isn't walking around switching his hips and calling his friends *girl*, then he can't be gay. I can take you to a gay bar where you'll see nothing but real manly men up in there. Men who you…" He flung his finger forward. "…would never know they were gay until you saw them there. That's exactly why there is this so-called 'epidemic' of down low men. Down low, my ass. Men have been fucking other men since the beginning of time; especially during the Roman Empire.

"Now, if you would've paid attention in your history class, you would've known this."

The room was silent for a moment.

"Touché to you, Ms. Lonnie."

Cara and Lonnie looked at me before erupting into laughter.

"O-kay," he added with a big smile.

"So how was work?" Tristan brought me back to where my mind should've been—in the here and now present with him.

"Work was work."

He gently massaged my shoulders. I rolled my head back, enjoying the feeling.

"You know my friends are teasing me. They're saying you must not be real, since they haven't met you yet."

He had yet to introduce me to anyone in his circle.

"Does it matter what they think? I mean, here I am in the flesh."

"And what beautiful flesh it is." He kissed me on the side of my neck and ran his hands from my shoulders down my arms into the water. Using his hands as cups, he scooped up water and let it rain down on my breasts.

"I'd like to show you off. Let them see what beauty really is." He kissed my neck again.

"You'll get a chance," I said, wondering how long I was going to be able to hide out, for fear of running into Octavia.

As much as I enjoyed the relationship that was developing with Tristan, there was always the thought of what I was going to do if we ran into her.

"Damn, woman. What are you doing to me? Got me coming straight home. No more sitting at the bar with the guys after work."

"The only reason you went to the bar was to meet women," I teased.

"You may be right; since we pretty much met in a bar."

"So, what you tryin' to say about me?"

"Maybe you were in the bar trying to meet somebody, too."

I playfully swatted his arm and pretended I was going to get out of the tub. He pulled me into him and began to tickle me.

"Okay, now. You're going to make me splash water out the tub."

I tried to move to the other end of the tub, but he pulled me back down on top of him.

"Tristan, don't get my hair wet."

"Stop worrying about your hair. If I wet it, I'll pay for a month of hairdos."

He kissed me gently at first. Lightly kissing the edges of my lips. Taking the time to suck ever so gently on them. Then the kiss became deep and full of passion.

"You do know how to drive me crazy, don't you?"

He ran his fingers gently down my arms.

"I like to think of it as pleasing you." His hands found their way around and down to my ass. Firmly gripping and massaging it. His hands began to travel further south. He slid the tip of his finger between my God-given slit until it found its planned destination—my clit. Applying pressure, he moved his finger in a quick motion. The stimulation was driving me crazy for real. My legs began to quiver as I gyrated my hips to heighten the pleasure of his touch.

"That's it, baby. Move with me."

He slipped a finger inside of me. I let out a gasp. He curved his finger inside me and moved it almost as fast as the finger on my clit.

It was a done deal. My body convulsed from the waist

down. My eyes were almost slits as my face contorted from the immense pleasure I was experiencing.

As if what he was doing wasn't enough, he leaned in and began to suck on my breasts. Teasing my nipples with his tongue, then taking as much breast as he could fit into his mouth. I didn't know how much more I would be able to take. My skin felt like it was on fire. Every nerve was on end.

"You there yet? You there, baby?"

"Yes, I'm there. I'm…" Before the next words passed over my lips, my legs locked up. I was no longer breathing, which heightened the tingling that began in my middle and was spreading to every other part of me.

"That's it, baby." He'd stopped suckling on my breast to watch the expression of pleasure on my face. His rock-hard dick was in his hand, being stroked in a slow up-and-down motion.

Being the sexually expressive person that I was, the volume of my incoherent moans was rising.

"Tristan," I whispered.

"I'm here, baby." The hand he'd used to bring me to this point was now underneath the water, down at his side. The other one was still working up and down his shaft.

I moved forward until I was hovering over him. He rubbed the head of his penis on my opening. I lowered myself onto him. It was my turn to watch him. Register the amount of pleasure I was bringing him.

"Oh damn," he moaned. "You feel so good."

The water sloshed back and forth with every move. I continued to ride him.

"Like that, baby?" I asked as I rotated my hips in a different motion.

"Ooh, yeah. That's the move right there, baby." He grabbed my hips to better direct my moves.

The lingering remains of my tingle started to build again.

"Damn, you're about to make me cum again." I grabbed hold to the sides of the tub and threw my head back.

"Get up and turn around," he commanded as he slipped from inside of me and forced me onto my feet. He turned me around so that he was behind me.

The entry was pure ecstasy. He came all the way out and rammed himself back up into me again. He repeated this over and over until neither one of us could hold out any longer.

"I'm about to cum, baby," he said, followed by a low grunt. His weight was on me and I realized it was all over for him. I was right behind him. The quivering of my legs caused me to slide down into the tub.

He moved away from me.

"You know how to put it on a brother."

"I thought you were putting it on me."

He grinned a little as he tried to catch his breath.

I got up and walked over to the shower stall.

"Who said I was finished?"

I looked at him. Leaning back against the tub, he could barely hold his head up on his shoulders.

"I think you need a little time to recuperate." I turned the water on for the shower and grabbed my towel from the rack on the other side of the room.

"So what's on the agenda for tonight?" I asked as I stepped into the flow of warm water.

"I was thinking we could swing by this birthday party for my homeboy."

I could hear the water move around in the tub as he stood to get out. He hit the level for the stopper.

"Is this a guy from work?"

"Since you haven't met any of my friends yet, I don't know how to explain him to you." He was standing at the sink, looking for his shaving tools.

"What's that supposed to mean?"

"Nothing, baby. Do you want to go or not?"

"What time does it start?"

He opened the shower door and startled me.

"You know, anytime you've ever asked me to come with you to a function, I've been there. No questions asked. Seems like every time I invite you to go with me to something that has to do with my friends, you always want to know when, where, why, or how long. What is it?"

I couldn't think of anything to say. I had dodged this bullet long enough. I knew meeting his friends was inevitable; especially since they were a tightly knit group like me and my girls. A much bigger group with girlfriends and wives included.

"Why are you trippin'? I only asked what time does it start?"

"You ask the same questions every time I invite you, only to tell me you have something else planned at the same time."

My entire body was covered in a white lather. I was beginning to get cold from him holding the door open. I took a deep breath and looked at him.

"That's not what I was going to say," I lied. "I wanted to know if I would have enough time to go home and get something nice to wear."

The frown on his half-shaven face was slowly replaced by a smile.

"We can stop by on our way there."

"Good. Now that we've got that settled, do you mind closing the door so I can finish?"

He leaned in and gave me a kiss, leaving remnants of his shaving cream behind on me. As I finished showering, I could hear him singing a little Chrisette Michele.

"If I have my way."

"Leave the singing to the professionals."

"You know you love my voice."

I smiled as I stuck my face beneath the water. He was right. The gravelly pitch was sexy as hell. Blew me away when he sung "All I Need Is Your Love"—an old Christopher Williams tune—to me one night. I was still smiling when I stepped out the shower.

"Damn, baby, why you rushing? I was about to come in there with you." He released the towel he had draped around his waist to reveal his dick, rock hard and at attention.

"Oh, you were about to *cum* alright. But, if we're going to get to this party at a decent hour, I think we need to pick this up later." I gave him a soft kiss before grabbing my towel to dry off.

"You know that's cold, right?" He was still standing with the shower door open.

"Cold like the water you need to shower in if you want to get that thing of yours to go down. Nice and cold." I winked at him and continued to dry off.

He looked down at his penis and then back at me, and shook his head.

"You might be right."

"Is your son still with your mom?" We did the majority of our hanging out at my house. T.J. seemed to always be with his mother. I had to respect his decision to see if this relationship was going somewhere before he got his son involved.

"That's his favorite place. It's only because my parents spoil him."

Typical grandparent stuff.

"Well, I hope I get to meet him soon."

He smiled at me.

"You will. I promise. Tonight, let's focus on you meeting my friends."

I was smiling on the outside, but inside I had an emotional storm going on.

CHAPTER 15

To say I was nervous would've been an extreme understatement. I had gone to the bathroom twice before we left my house.

"Girl, go and have a good time and don't worry about it. It's been a couple of months now; she may not remember you. You met with her for what? All of five or ten minutes?"

"I know, it's just—"

"Stop worrying."

That was the conversation I had with Ebonee before leaving. I played it over in my head as we stood on the doorstep of his friend's house.

"You okay?"

I looked at him and nodded my head. He gave my hand a light squeeze before ringing the doorbell. A few seconds later a guy appeared at the door. With wire-framed glasses and shoulder-length locks, he was a few inches shorter than Tristan.

"It's about time you got here, Negro." He gave Tristan a strong handshake and pulled him in for an embrace.

"Whatever. I said I was coming."

"You've been saying that a lot lately, but for some reason, you never seem to show up."

I was standing quietly behind Tristan as they continued their playful banter. My mind began to wonder about my appearance. *Was I dressed nice enough? Was my hair in place still? Did I still have on lipstick?* I squeezed the clutch in my hand tightly.

"Oh, damn, this…" Tristan reached for my hand and pulled me beside him, "…is Deeva."

I quickly pasted a smile on my face.

He slowly let his gaze travel my entire length. A dull, unenthused look was masked when he stuck out his hand to shake mine.

"It's nice to finally meet his mystery woman. I take it you're the reason we haven't seen much of him lately?"

"Back down, man. It's not even like that."

He released my hand from the half-hearted handshake he'd offered. Tristan placed his hand around my waist and took a defensive stand.

He stepped to the side to allow us to enter.

"Everybody is out back." The music led the way. A large group of people were out through the glass doors, on the deck and near the pool area.

"You do realize you never told me your friend's name?"

Tristan smiled and acknowledged people as we walked by them.

"Damn, baby. I'm sorry. That was Lorenzo."

"Oh, the one who wants you to date his girlfriend's friend? Now I understand the reception I got."

He squeezed my hand a little as a reassuring gesture.

"And here she comes now."

My heart began to race a little. I didn't know what this scene was going to be like, but I knew it wouldn't be good. When she saw me with him, I was sure she was going to think something shady had happened. I searched my mind for what I was going to say, but I was drawing a blank.

"Deeva, this is Fallon." He moved out the way so I had a clear view of her.

"Oh, so you're Deeva," she said in a sugary, sweet-laced voice. She held four fingers limply out in front of me, like she was expecting me to kiss her damn hand or something.

"It's nice to meet you, too," I said as I shook the fingers.

"Tristan, it feels like it's been ages since we've seen you."

"I've been busy."

"I can see." She looked me up and down.

"Where's everybody else?"

I glanced around and wondered why he'd asked that.

"You know your boys like to hit the table."

"I thought I'd find them in the basement. We're going to go down and say hello."

"Deeva, you're welcome to stay up here. That room is probably filled with cigar smoke and dirty jokes. No place for a woman."

I looked at Tristan.

"I think I'll take her with me. You know, so I can introduce her to everyone." He gave her a friendly peck on her cheek before heading back into the house. We made our way down the basement stairs into exactly what Fallon had described; a thick cloud of smoke and the sound of men going back and forth as two of them engaged in a competitive game of eight ball while the others were seated at a table in the corner playing a hand of Spades. The latter being one of my favorites.

"Hey, hey now. Watch your mouths. There's a lady in our midst," Tristan announced as we came deeper into the room.

All movement stopped as every head in the room turned toward us.

"Could it be? No, no. Wes, didn't you say you were going to put out an APB on this niggah right here?"

"Deeva, this joker here is—"

"Quincy." He bowed in front of me and grabbed my hand and kissed it.

"Aw, damn. Ya'll see Q over there trying to act like he's a Casanova or something?"

"Man, forget you, Malik."

"Let's see, that's Jackson and Fred on the table." They both nodded their heads at me.

"Wes, Delante, Kelvin, and Malik are over there in the corner." Each one of them raised their hands as he called out their names.

"So you're Deeva?"

I nodded my head and smiled.

"Ooh, a pretty smile."

"Alright, chill out, Q."

"I'm only giving you your props, man. She is beautiful. I see why you've been staying away."

"I've only missed what? Three events ya'll have had."

"Niggah, we ain't seen you in a month of Sundays. Talking about three events."

"Q, that means I've only missed four. Wow, one more than what I said."

Lorenzo came up behind us and handed Tristan a beer.

"Thought you'd like one of these. Deeva, I'm sorry, but I didn't bring you anything since I'm not sure what you like."

"I'll take one of those, if it's not a bother."

He pulled his lips in and shook his head.

"Another Heineken coming up."

"Bring me one while you're at it," Quincy called.

Lorenzo shot him a nasty look.

"So, Deeva, right?"

I nodded.

"What do you do? Where do you live? Where do you work?"

"We know who you working," someone chimed in and the room filled with laughter.

Tristan shook his head.

"Don't mind them, baby. They're all crazy," he said

loudly. "Especially this nosey fool right here." He tapped Quincy on the chest.

"Ain't nobody in here crazy. Deeva, can you believe some of us have been friends since junior high school? That's what? More than twenty years."

"Wow! That's a long time."

"What about you? You have any girlfriends you've had since at least high school?"

"Yeah. I have three I'm still really close with. One of them I've known since kindergarten."

"Damn! Kindergarten? So how many years is that?"

"Niggah, didn't your mama ever teach you it's not polite to ask a woman her age."

"Whatever, Action Jackson."

"Deeva, you can cuss him out if you want," Jackson added as Fred bent down to hit his next ball. "I'll give you one of these sticks to do it." He reached over toward the rack on the wall where four more sticks were hanging.

"That's okay. I'm about to turn thirty soon."

"You're thirty?"

I nodded again.

"Fellas, do ya'll believe this woman is about to turn thirty?" Quincy asked the room.

I didn't know if he was saying it in a good way or a bad one.

"Thirty? Man, I was about to tease Tristan about robbing the cradle."

Tristan slid behind me and wrapped his arms around

me. like he was proud of all the compliments his boys were showering on me.

"Here you go." Lorenzo handed me an unopened bottle.

"Damn, you could've brought her a glass to pour it in."

"That's okay. I'm good, Quincy." I looked at Lorenzo and tipped my head toward him to say thank you.

"Where can I find a bottle opener?"

"There's one over on the bar." Lorenzo pointed to the area of the room he'd just come from. I could feel a bit of tension in the room as I walked over to search for the opener.

"Where's mine?" I heard Quincy ask.

"Over there in the fridge waiting for you to come and get it, I guess."

"You need to stop being evil, you know."

I found the opener on the bar. The fridge was near, so I grabbed Quincy a cold one and opened it for him before rejoining them.

"Here you go." I handed the cold beer to Quincy.

"Thank you, beautiful." He shot a look over to Lorenzo, who was staring at me now.

I turned the bottle up and took a few swallows.

"This hits the spot." I held the beer up to Tristan.

"That's game," someone shouted from the table in the corner. "Who's next? Who thinks they can handle stepping into the ring with the champs?" Delante asked as Wes and Kelvin left the table.

"Baby, you want to show them how it's really done?"

Tristan asked. He'd gone with me to a Spades tournament at Ebonee's house one night and knew I was a serious player.

"Of course. That is, if the fellas don't mind a lady joining the game." I batted my eyes and smiled at them.

"Oh, yeah. This one is in the bag, my man," Delante said to Malik.

Tristan and I sat down at the table.

"Are we just playing or are we playing for *something*?" I asked. I placed my clutch on the table.

"Damn, she sat down talking shit."

"What would you like to do, pretty lady?" Delante smiled at me.

I looked at Tristan for advice. He nodded his head and shrugged his shoulders. I opened my clutch.

"She's serious, too." Quincy came closer to the table.

I saw Jackson nudge Fred and they came closer.

"Let me see what I've got in here." I pulled out my wallet. I began to count off the twenties I had in my wallet. "I got about two hundred. Is that enough?" I was baiting them on.

They began to rummage in their pants pockets in a rushed manner.

"I got eighty. What about you, Malik?"

"Man, I got a hundred."

"One of ya'll give us twenty. You know your money is safe with us at the helm," said Delante.

Less than an hour later, I was two hundred dollars richer.

"Where'd you find her, Tristan?"

"Next time you can be my partner, Deeva," Quincy said.

"Sit down somewhere. You don't have the first idea about playing this game."

"Next time you and I can run the table, Deeva. Hell, you know they have Spades tournaments now? We can sign up for that." Delante shook my hand.

"This was fun, gentlemen." I reached for Malik's hand after I let go of Delante's. "I hope there are no hard feelings behind this."

They all laughed and joined me and Tristan as we walked back upstairs to find something to eat.

"I'm going to run to the bathroom. I'll meet you in the kitchen." He kissed me before walking off in the other direction.

I walked back to the deck where we'd been earlier. I spied Lorenzo talking to Fallon. I knew I wasn't a welcome fixture in their home, but I would endure the remainder of the night for Tristan.

"You're alright with me, Deeva," Quincy said.

"Hey. I was trying to find something to eat."

"Come on. I'll take you to the kitchen where all the food is."

I followed him back into the house.

"The plates are over there, along with forks and napkins. You'll learn that Ms. Fallon likes to lay out a lavish spread at all her events. To her credit, she's got a great caterer."

I laughed and slapped him on the shoulder.

"Not everyone has time to cook."

"When you don't work, you should." He gave me a look.

I loaded up my plate with a little bit of everything and headed back outside to find a place to sit.

"Deeva?"

I looked up and damn near choked on the meatball I'd just placed in my mouth.

"I wasn't sure if that was you or not."

"Octavia, right?"

"Yes. I'm sorry. I know you probably have a bunch of clients who come through your doors."

"I don't meet all of them."

"Then I feel honored." She sat down at the table with me.

I gulped down the cup of spiked punch.

"I didn't get a chance to thank you for your work. What's your assistant's name?"

"Cara."

"Yes, Cara. Her words really helped open my eyes and see I wasn't in a relationship at all. So, thank you for your help."

"You're welcome." I picked at a piece of stuffed chicken roll.

"Who are you here with?" She looked around.

"Oh, I was invited by a friend who's friends with a friend of the birthday boy."

"Oh, okay. Well, I'm not going to hold you up any

longer. Maybe I'll run into you again before the party is over."

"Maybe…"

"See you later," she called as she got up and walked away.

As soon as she was out of sight, I got up and threw my plate in the trash and headed for the door. I searched in my purse for my cell.

"You okay, Deeva?" Quincy startled me. I stared at him. "You look like you've seen a ghost."

"I'm fine. I need to get something from the car. If you see Tristan, tell him I went to the car."

"Okay," he said with a puzzled look on his face.

I rushed past him to the front door and down the driveway to the street. I couldn't get to the car fast enough. Once there, I remembered we were in Tristan's car. I began to dial his number again on my cell. After four tries, he finally answered.

"Where are you?"

"I'm at the car. I know you want to be here for your boy's birthday, but I need to get home."

"What's wrong, baby? Did something happen?"

I could tell from the difference in sounds coming through his phone that he was on the move and headed my way.

"Something personal I need to see about, but you don't have to leave. I called Ebonee and she said she'll pick me up."

"Called Ebonee? Why? If you have to go, I have to go."

"Don't, Tristan. Your friends—"

"I'm almost at the car." He hung up the phone.

I could hear the rhythm of his footsteps as he got closer. The alarm beeped, unlocking the car doors. He walked over to the passenger side, where I was leaning against the car, and opened the door for me.

"Come on. I'll get you home."

My arms were tucked tightly underneath my breasts as I fought with what I was going to do and say to him about the situation.

He was about to walk around to the other side of the car. I caught him by the arm.

"Tristan, you don't have to leave. I'll call—"

"Baby, I know you're uncomfortable. I've caught the lil' slights you've gotten from the host and hostess." He tilted my chin up to face him. "Don't you know you're important to me? If you're uncomfortable, then we're out of here. Simple as that." He softly kissed my lips, then ushered me into the car.

He slowly pulled away from the curb and rode back by the house on our way out of the subdivision. Just as we passed by, I caught sight of Fallon and Lorenzo standing on the porch talking to Octavia.

I was going to have to tell him before they did. I had a feeling if they told him the story, it was going to come back as something else, and I didn't want that.

CHAPTER 16

"I know you were about to shit bricks, Ms. Thang." Lonnie handed me a cup of coffee and sat in what had become his assigned seat in my office.

"It was a harrowing moment, to say the least?"

"What, bitch?"

I laughed.

"I want to know how his friends acted toward you." Cara hadn't opened one folder on her lap.

"For the most part, they were cool. Well, not all of them. The one whose party it was and whose girl is friends with Octavia, he didn't even try to pretend like he was feeling me. Lorenzo."

"He sounds like he got a lil' *bitchassness* in him. Maybe we need to put one of my girls on him and see."

Cara and I burst into laughter at Lonnie's use of Puffy's new coined phrase of the year.

"Ya'll laughing, but I have brought you more than enough proof that these Negroes are serious about this DL stuff. Hmm, girl, he may be interested in your man for himself and that's why he wants to keep your man so tightly in his loop."

"Shut up, Lonnie. I didn't get that vibe from him."

"Oh, so you're an expert on it? Then you must not need me anymore."

"Don't go drama up in here, queen," Cara said to him.

"Lonnie, you know you're an asset to my company."

"Plus, we know how much you love to hear us tell you. So, there's the quota for the day," Cara said.

"Deeva, I don't know why you keep this mean bitch around."

Cara jacked back at him playfully.

"Girl, you know my reflexes are quick."

"Okay, you two. I thought you were here to help me?"

"What are you going to do? I think you should tell him. You'd already met him—and spent the weekend with him—before she even walked into the office."

"But he's not going to see it that way. See, men don't like to feel like they've been set up. Even if you catch them in the wrong, they'll flip the script on you. Before you know it, you'll be apologizing for even looking into his cheating-ass ways."

"Lonnie, Tristan is not that way."

He rolled his eyes at Cara.

"And how would you know? He's Deeva's man; not yours."

"I can tell by the way he looks at Deeva. He acts like he can't get enough of her."

"Yeah, until he finds out she's been keeping secrets from him."

"I say don't tell him."

"I say you do what you feel you have to do, Deeva. You know him better than either one of us. So, do what you feel is right." Cara rolled her eyes back at Lonnie.

I thought about what they'd both said.

"I need to think about it more before I make any real decisions."

"That's what I'm saying, girl. If it ain't broke, don't fix it."

"Just don't let his friends tell him before you do. You'll never be able to bounce back from that hurt."

CHAPTER 17

Tristan's car was in my driveway when I got in. My nerves began to act like they'd been plugged in. I racked my brain, trying to remember if he'd told me he was coming over earlier.

"Hey, baby," I said as I opened the front door.

"Hey." He kissed me.

"Is something wrong?" I placed my bags on the sofa as I tried to appear unnerved. I nonchalantly flipped through my mail.

"No. Why?"

"I wasn't expecting you to be here, is all. I thought we were meeting at your house?"

"Well, something came up and I want you to go somewhere with me."

If I had been facing him, the look of worry on my face would've gone up like a red flag. Never turning to face him, I walked into the kitchen and grabbed a glass from the cabinet.

"Come on, baby. You don't even have to change."

"Where are we going?"

"If I tell you, then it won't be a surprise."

I quickly gulped down the glass of water I'd gotten from the fridge. I was going for a second glass when he came up behind me.

"We've got people waiting on us. I'll get you all the water you want when we get where we're going." He placed the glass on the counter and grabbed me by the hand.

"People waiting on us?"

"See, you've made me give away part of my surprise." He continued to lead me to the door.

I grabbed my purse from the sofa and followed him, protesting as we went.

"If we're meeting people, I need to comb my hair and freshen up a bit."

"Baby, you look fine. Stop worrying."

Stop worrying? At that moment, it seemed impossible to do. Different scenarios ran through my mind. Lorenzo, Fallon, and Octavia were more than likely the people waiting for us. Waiting to confront me. To accuse me of deliberately sabotaging Octavia and Tristan's relationship.

For the first time since I'd opened my business, I regretted getting into it. Wondered how many clients had regretted acquiring my services; especially those with unfavorable outcomes. *Had I been unknowingly ruining people's lives?*

"What's wrong?" Tristan grabbed my hand and squeezed it.

"Nothing. I was thinking about something that happened at work."

He shook his head and continued to drive.

"Ah, the wonderful world of advertising. Want to talk about it?" He never took his eyes off the road.

I sat quietly and continued to look out the window. The battle of whether to tell him or not weighed heavily. His silence was fuel to the fire, which seemed to confirm he knew something. At least, in my mind it did.

Deciding to come clean, I took a deep breath and looked at him.

"Tristan…"

"We're here, baby." He pulled into a driveway and put the car in PARK. He turned and looked at me. He seemed to stare at me like he was looking for something.

I couldn't will my mouth to move. My brain was screaming, "I need to tell you something!" but my lips wouldn't move.

He smiled and got out the car.

I sat still. Looking at the empty spot where he had been.

"Come on, baby. They're waiting on us."

Slowly, I followed. As we stood on the porch waiting for some- one to answer the door, I felt as if I was going to stand in front of a firing squad. Not once did I pay attention to my surroundings until the door opened.

"Tristan! Hey, baby," said an older woman's voice.

He stood in the doorframe and gave her a hug. She stepped to the side so he could enter.

"Mama, I have someone I want you to meet." He held his hand back and pulled me in the door.

I smiled and was immediately embraced in a loving hug.

"Hello, Deeva." She continued to hug me and pat my back. "I was wondering when he was going to bring you, so I could meet you. I've heard so much about you." She let me go and held me out in front of her, so she could get a good look at me.

"Tristan, she's beautiful. Inside and out. You know, Mama knows." She gave him a look to confirm it.

"Come on in here." She held my hand and led me down to the basement.

I could hear a voice and then a chorus of laughter.

"You need to quit, Daddy."

"Hey, everybody. Look who's here."

All talking ceased and their heads turned toward us.

Mrs. Savage led the way, with Tristan and me in tow.

"Hey, boy," the older man, who I knew from sight alone was Tristan's father, said, "It's about time you got here. Bring that pretty girl over here, so I can get a better look."

Tristan grabbed my hand and introduced me to everyone we passed as we made our way over to his father. He had two sisters, Talia and Thomasina; and two brothers, Junior—Thomas, Jr., who was the oldest—and Tallmadge. Each one of them greeted me as if they'd known me forever.

"Deeva, this here is—"

"I can introduce myself. I don't need you to do it for me. I'm Thomas Savage, Sr." He stuck out his hand for a proper handshake.

"It's nice to meet you, Mr. Savage."

"Where's T.J.?" Tristan asked.

"You know that boy is upstairs, probably glued in front of that game. I'll go get him."

"I got it, Mama." Tristan kissed me on the cheek and ran off toward the stairs.

The rest of the family continued to entertain me as I waited for his return.

"We're going to have dinner in a minute. I hope you brought your appetite with you," Mrs. Savage informed me.

The family resemblance was strong between Mr. Savage and his children. There was no way he'd ever be on a talk show contesting the paternity of any of them. All the boys had his same stature. None of them under six feet two. Tristan being the tallest of them at six-four.

"So, how long have you been seeing Tristan?"

"Thomasina, don't interrogate the girl."

"I'm not interrogating her, Mama. We all want to know. Go on upstairs and make sure none of your pots are burning," she said in a light, playful tone.

"We've been dating almost four months."

"Four months?"

"Stay out of your brother's business, Junior."

"You know Tristan is her baby."

Just then, Tristan reappeared.

"Are they hassling you, baby?"

I smiled and shook my head no.

"They're just asking routine questions."

"See, Mama, even she knows these are normal questions people ask," Thomasina responded.

"Deeva, I have somebody else I want you to meet." Tristan looked up the stairs. "Come on down here, boy."

A few seconds later, a miniature version of Tristan slowly made his way down the stairs. Apprehensively, he approached me and reached to shake my hand.

"I'm T.J."

"T.J., it's nice to meet you. I'm Deeva."

"Oh, my daddy really likes you." He smiled as he looked over to Tristan. "She's pretty, Daddy."

Everyone in the room laughed. I could feel the heat settling in my cheeks.

"Told you your old man had good taste," Tristan responded as he kissed me on the cheek.

"The food is ready," Mrs. Savage called down.

As everyone else made their way up the stairs, Tristan pulled me to the side.

"So, what do you think? Think you could see yourself putting up with these folks on a couple of holidays a year? Maybe a Sunday dinner, once or twice a month?"

"I could definitely see that." I put my arms around his neck.

"Good. Good," he said as he kissed me.

"Daddy, Grandma says for you and Ms. Deeva to come on up these stairs before she comes down and gets you."

Tristan kissed me one last time before we joined everyone else.

It was a night to remember. I felt as if I'd found a home as I sat and enjoyed the stories that flowed endlessly throughout dinner. Yeah, I could definitely get used to this.

CHAPTER 18

Tristan sat on the edge of his bed and stared at the velvet box. He hadn't been sure of many things in his life, but he was sure about this. Taking this step was as big a step any man would take in his life. He didn't want to spend another day without her. He knew he wanted to wake up to her every morning and watch her fall asleep every night.

"Yeah, it's time to do this," he said to his reflection.

After introducing her to his family two months earlier, he knew she was the one. Not because she clicked so well with everyone, but because his mother, who had been right about each one of her children's mates, told him so. Her words were with him now as he thought about the night he had taken her home.

"Baby, that girl there is your soul mate. She's the one God made especially for you." She continued to wash the dishes as he helped out by drying them.

"You think so, Ma?" He had a smile of satisfaction on his face.

"Think so? I know so, Son. Look at you. You round

here smiling for no reason. Just the thought of her makes you happy."

His mother was right. Whenever he thought about Deeva, he would get this feeling inside that felt like sunshine was running through his veins.

"So, when you plan on asking her?"

"Asking her what?"

She gave him a sideways glance.

"Okay. You can play dumb if you want to. The only reason you brought her here tonight was because you wanted us to meet her before you asked her to marry you."

"Oh, Mama, you put too much into stuff. I just thought it was time for her to meet the family. We've been dating for a good while." He stacked the dried dishes neatly in the drainer she had on the counter.

"I put too much into stuff. Okay."

Neither one said another word before they were interrupted by the elder Mr. Savage entering the kitchen.

"Still hanging on to your mama's apron strings?"

Tristan laughed.

"So, when you gonna ask that girl in there to marry you?"

Mrs. Savage stopped watching and looked at Tristan.

"And you said I'm putting too much into it."

Tristan smiled again as he thought about how well she'd blended with his family. From his parents to his siblings and everyone else—she was a hit at the family reunion they'd attended a month ago.

Now he was faced with the daunting task of making this memorable moment. A moment so special she'd tell the story to anyone who was willing to listen. Special enough that she'd say yes without any hesitation.

He picked up his cell and called Ebonee.

"Hey, I need to recruit you for something."

He filled her in and took the few pointers she offered. They'd planned everything out to happen that night.

"Thanks for your help. I'll see you later."

He flipped the velvet box open once more. The one-carat diamond in a platinum setting gleamed. It was worth every penny he'd spent.

"I know she's going to love this," he thought as he closed the box.

If he was going to have everything ready and in place for tonight, he needed to get a move on. There were a few things he'd have to pick up. Ebonee would handle everything else.

"God, please let this woman say yes."

"T.J., I need to talk to you."

Not too happy about being called away from playing his favorite game, T.J. took his time. "Yes, Daddy."

"I need to talk to you about something. Come. Have a seat."

T.J. gave him a strange look before obeying.

"We've been spending a lot of time with Deeva. I was wondering what you think about her becoming my wife."

"That's cool."

"You know that means she'll live in the house with us. We'll have to give up our bachelor pad, but we'd be getting a really great addition to our family."

"Dad, I really like Deeva. She's funny, plus she likes to play my game with me."

"I'm going to ask her tonight, so I need you to do a few things for me. The first one is, go take your shower so we can get dressed."

"I'm going with you?" There was a hint of excitement in his voice.

"Tonight, you get to help good ol' dad." Tristan patted his son on the back.

"You know, with me being as cute as I am, you have a better chance of her saying yes." T.J. popped his collar as he strode past his dad.

Tristan playfully slapped him on the butt with the towel he had on the bed.

"Okay, Your Cuteness. Don't forget where you got your good looks from."

They horsed around a minute more before Tristan sent T.J. off to shower.

Ebonee would arrive in an hour with her part. He needed to get going so he'd be ready.

CHAPTER 19

"So, what are your plans for tonight, boss lady?"

"My man is cooking dinner tonight."

"Ooh, that sounds romantic."

"Yeah. We'll probably end up watching a movie or two after we're finished."

Cara pointed toward the Apple Store.

"Girl, I got this damn thing and have no idea how to work it." She dug in her purse and retrieved the red iPod Nano she'd gotten from Carey; her Christmas fling.

"You've been walking around with that thing in your purse for three months."

"I know, but you know how it is. The New Year brings more responsibilities and more things to do and before you know it, you're halfway through the year."

We walked into the store and were greeted by one of their eager staff members. He checked us in and gave us an appointment at the Genius Bar.

"This is so cool. The setup is really nice and they have a trained staff to help you with anything." We continued to walk deeper into the store where we found the Genius Bar at the halfway point.

"Look, there's your name." I pointed to one of the two huge monitors on the wall behind the bar.

"See, this is what I'm talking about. This is taking your business to the next level."

We'd been talking about expanding; possibly opening up our services to men who wanted to see if their women were potential cheaters. I was still uncertain about it. The whole idea of my company was to be a tool for women, but I knew all too well that women were capable of being cheaters also.

Cara had suggested we have traveling seminars where we would teach women how to notice the signs of when they were being cheated on and what to do.

"Before we decide to do anything, we need to sit down and come up with a business plan and narrow down our ideas." I walked over to one of the many computers on display.

"I've always wanted to get an Apple system. I've heard they're better than a regular computer system."

"If you're planning to do creative stuff, they are."

"Cara, they're about to call your name." I pointed again to the board.

"Did Tristan say what he's cooking tonight? And can he cook?"

"Yes, my baby can cook."

"Your baby? Umm, that's some real progress there."

Before I could respond, her name was called. I continued to browse around the store while she got the help she needed.

"Deeva, right?"

I turned and was practically face-to-face with Fallon. It had been quite some time since Tristan and I had attended the event at their house. After the cold reception I'd received, he had never brought up the subject about us hanging out with them again. Occasionally, Quincy, Jackson, Wes, and Delante would come and hang out with us. Fred and Malik were the married two in the crew, so we rarely saw them.

"Hi. How are you?" I asked with as much enthusiasm as I could muster up.

"I'm good. How's Tristan? We haven't seen much of him lately. You seem to keep him pretty busy."

I knew she didn't mean her remark in a nice way, but I wasn't about to let her get underneath my skin.

"I wouldn't say that."

"How's business lately?"

I tried not to let the surprise of her question register in my eyes.

"Business is good. Really good, actually."

"That's good to hear." She switched her oversized gold bag to her other shoulder.

The awkwardness of the moment seemed to increase by the second.

"I thought your name sounded familiar. I mean, how many people are walking around here named Deeva? I know some people like to call themselves one, but not many actually have the name on their birth certificates. So, when I saw Octavia talking to you, I began to wonder how she knew you. Well, being the inquisitive person that I am, I asked. And you want to know what she told me?"

I smirked at her. I refused to give her the satisfaction she was in search of.

"I could only imagine."

"I bet. I wonder if Tristan knows he was reeled in because he was part of an investigation."

"See, that's where you're wrong. If you weren't so busy trying to hook up all your friends with your boyfriend's friends, you would've realized Tristan wasn't interested in your girlfriend and you could've saved her some time and money."

"You don't know me. You don't—"

"Oh, but I do know you. I know women like you all too well. Things in their relationship aren't as solid as they'd like for everyone to believe, so what do they do? They try to make the circle as tight as possible by setting their man's friends up with their own friends. This way the boyfriend looks at how well everyone is clicking with one another and decides the relationship is worth the work. Far be it for him to be the one to break up the nice tight circle that has been formed.

"Instead of worrying about what's going on with me and Tristan, maybe you should see why your man has yet to commit to biting the bullet with you after a three-year engagement. Yeah, I know about it.

"Now, if you'll excuse me, I think my girlfriend is ready to go." I walked away from her as Cara got closer.

"Who is that?" Cara gave Fallon a warning glance.

"That's Fallon. The bitch I told you about."

"Is she threatening you?" Cara was in ass-kicking mode all the time.

"I'm not worried about her. If anything, she needs to be worried about me." I pulled my phone from my purse. It was time to fight fire with fire. I knew Fallon wasn't going to lie down and take this one on the chin. She probably had her phone to her ear already, telling Lorenzo what had transpired. Going on and on about how he needed to tell Tristan about me. So, I would have to be ready and have a lil' something up my sleeve.

"Lonnie. Hey, babes. Got something I need you to do for me."

CHAPTER 20

"Hey, baby." Tristan kissed me on the cheek.

"You know you didn't have to drive over here to get me. Now you're going to have to bring me home tonight, instead of me spending the night and leaving to come home to get ready for work. If I had driven my car, I could've stayed until morning."

"Can I be in charge tonight? Sit back and let me handle what's going to happen. If we end up falling asleep and I have to get up early and take you home, then I'll get up and take you home. Tonight, I want you to relax." He kissed me before turning the corner.

"I thought we were going to your house for dinner. Did you change your mind?" I looked at our evening attire. He'd called earlier and told me we were going somewhere nice, so dress accordingly and it had to either be red or have red in it. After an hour of laying out outfit after outfit, I finally decided on the red, one shoulder, floor-length gown I'd only worn once.

"You look really handsome tonight." I grabbed his hand.

He flashed me his kilowatt smile.

"You already know you are stunning."

"Your tie matches my dress." I fingered his tie. It was a nice contrast to his all-black ensemble.

I was surprised when we pulled up to his house.

"Did you forget something?"

"Yeah. You might as well come in 'cause it might take me a minute." He jumped out the car and ran around to open the door for me. Before we reached the porch, the door opened. There stood T.J. dressed identical to his dad.

"Welcome. We have a very special evening planned for you. Won't you please follow me? Your dinner awaits you."

Obediently, Tristan and I followed our host for the evening. The lighting in the house was dimmed; candles served as the main source of lighting. The setting was serene. I could hear soft jazz being pumped throughout the house via the intercom system.

The table was beautifully set for two.

"Madame." T.J. waited for me to move my hands out the way. He gently placed my napkin in my lap.

"You're not going to join us?"

He smiled.

"No, I'll be having my dinner in the kitchen." He walked out.

"Tristan, let that baby have dinner with us."

"Like I said earlier, I'm in control. Enjoy everything we've planned and relax."

T.J. entered the room with a bottle of wine. He showed it to both of us and awaited our approval. Tristan gave him a nod and he left the bottle on the table near him and walked out again.

Tristan poured both of us a glass and picked his up and raised it.

"To the most beautiful woman I know." He tapped my glass with his.

I began to blush.

The rest of dinner went great. We were enjoying an after-dinner chat when T.J. came in to recruit his dad for something.

"I'll be right back, baby." Tristan kissed me before leaving the room.

I must have sat there for close to ten minutes before I heard Tristan's voice on the intercom.

"Baby, can you come into the family room?"

As I reached the family room, I was shocked to find T.J. standing in the middle of the room. There were balloons everywhere. There must have been ten dozen roses strategically placed. The room had been romantically decorated. Red and silver streamers fell from the ceiling. I could feel tears well up in my eyes.

Suddenly I heard Tristan's voice, but T.J. was still the only one in the room. When I got closer, I noticed T.J.'s mouth was moving. He was lip-synching his father's words.

"From the first time I saw you, I felt an instant connection. While I wasn't expecting to find love, that's exactly what I found. Every time I look into your eyes, I feel as if I can get lost in them forever. So…" T.J. got down on one knee.

I had to place my hand over my mouth to keep my lips from trembling. The tears that had begun to well up spilled down my cheeks.

Tristan entered the room and joined T.J.

"We're asking you to love us forever. We promise to honor and cherish you for the rest of our days. We can't say we won't get on your nerves at times, but we're willing to put in the work for our family. I want to share everything with you. My mornings. My nights."

Suddenly Tristan got up and reached into his pocket.

"Deeva McCoy, I love you and if you'll have me and my son, nothing will make me happier. Will you marry me?" He popped open the velvet box and presented the ring to me.

I looked over at T.J., who seemed to be holding his breath. I placed my hand on the side of Tristan's face and kissed him.

"Yes."

"Yes?"

"Yes. Yes."

"She said yes!" Tristan kissed me hard and long.

T.J. came and stood next to us. I gave him a kiss.

"You really mean it?"

"I sure do."

He threw his arms around my waist and hugged me tight.

The three of us stood embracing one another.

"Oh, here." Tristan pulled the ring out the box and placed it on my finger.

I held out my hand and looked it over. It was the most beautiful thing I'd ever seen.

"It's only the beginning, baby. Only the beginning."

CHAPTER 21

"Let me see that thing again." Lonnie grabbed my hand and pretended he was putting on something special to give my ring a closer look.

"Oh, yes. He definitely gets an A-plus on this. This is platinum and at least one carat."

"Boy, how can you tell that by looking at it?"

"Ms. Cara, I have been trying to school you since day one. You have to know things that are important. Like the grade of the diamond is more important than the size. When you study certain things, you learn to recognize them by sight alone."

"Thank you for the life lesson." Cara turned back to me.

We'd been discussing the entire run-in with Fallon from the other day.

"You need to sit him down and tell him everything. I know you've got your secret weapon over there working on something, but you really need to beat them to the punch. If they get their punch off first, that's going to be a hard blow."

"Aren't we all philosophical?"

"Lonnie, don't start with your *kiss but don't tell* theory."

"Sometimes we shouldn't tell everything."

Cara looked up at the ceiling and then back over to me.

"Cara, I've decided to tell him everything. About my business. About meeting Octavia. Everything. I plan to spend the rest of my life with this man. I love him and his love means more to me than all the money I'll ever make. Besides, I wouldn't give that bitch and her hen-pecked man the satisfaction of having something over me."

Lonnie slapped my hand.

"You go, gurl!" He snapped his fingers.

"Good. This way, you'll have a good start."

Ebonee breezed into the office.

"Hello, ladies." She paused and looked at Lonnie.

"Hello to you, too, beautiful." He walked over to her and they air-kissed each other on both cheeks.

"See, I didn't know what mood you were in today. Some days you're in sistah-girl mode, and then others you're being a lil' butch."

"You have never seen me act butch. Stop that lying."

We all laughed. There was nothing butch about Lonnie.

"Where's Lisa?" I looked behind Ebonee.

"She told me she was going to meet me here."

"Now see, she's the first one to have an attitude if things are chosen and she doesn't have any input."

Lonnie picked up his schedule book. "Why do you need her input? It's your wedding."

"Because Deeva has always been one to try and please

everyone. Now see me, on the other hand, I could not care less about pleasing people."

Lonnie winked at Ebonee. "I knew there was a reason I liked you."

"Since I'm the biggest of them all, I should have the last say on what dress is chosen for us."

Lisa walked into the room and everyone stopped talking.

"I guess I was the subject, since you all got quiet." She dropped her purse on the table along with her jacket.

"Umm, Ms. Thang, don't you know the bottom of your purse is one of the dirtiest things? I bet you just picked it up from the floor of your car."

"And?"

"And you come in here and throw it on the table where I eat my lunch? How rude is that?" Lonnie placed her purse in an extra chair in the corner.

This was definitely going to be a lively group to deal with. Lonnie was in charge of the planning. He was free, but he was also good at organizing and getting people to do what they're supposed to do. It would be one less headache for me to deal with.

"Here's the bridesmaid dress. It should work well for everyone. These are the shoes. I need to get everyone's shoe size, so I can hurry up and order them and have them dyed. Ebonee, your dress will be slightly different in color and the front will be different." Lonnie handed everyone a copy.

The dress, long and slightly off the shoulders, was simple but elegant. With just enough cleavage, it would complement any shape.

"Any objections?" Lonnie looked around the table. "Good. Deeva, this is a copy of the invitation. I think it's classy, but definitely in the budget."

He handed me a box. I opened it and found a scroll with a sample wedding announcement on it.

"Ooh, Lonnie. This is really nice. Tristan is going to love this."

Ebonee and Cara crowded around me to have a look. "Where did you find these?"

"You know me. I have my ways." He winked and kept talking.

"Here is the schedule for everything. There will be three rehearsals. The final one will be followed by the rehearsal dinner, which I think we'll be able to have at a good friend of mine's house."

"Is this the same house you're talking about having the actual wedding?"

"Yes, it is. I'm going to call her tonight and see if we can use the area out by the pool. She has a really nice area with an outdoor kitchen and more than enough room to seat at least fifty people."

"You are really on top of things, aren't you?" Lisa asked in a not-so-complimenting tone. I thought I even saw her roll her neck a little. I wasn't worried though. Lonnie would get her in check, if need be.

She and I hadn't really talked since the blow-up on the

night I met Tristan. I tried to call her, but she claimed she was working or doing something else each time.

"Deeva, here are packets for your other bridesmaids. You can give it to them when you see them. I need to get everyone's measurements so I can order the dresses. It takes about four to six weeks to get them. This gives us enough time to get them and do any alterations, if someone needs them.

"Ladies, the three of you are her best friends so more will be expected of you than the other bridesmaids. If I call and ask you to do something, please work with me in order to get it done." He pulled out his BlackBerry and turned to Lisa.

"Sweetheart, I need to get your number." He looked and waited for her to rattle off the numbers.

She hesitated for a breath and looked at him, like he'd cursed her out.

"Look, what the fuck is your problem?" I asked her.

"What?!" she exclaimed.

"Lisa, I have been trying my best to ignore the childish bullshit you've been exhibiting. If you have something you want to get off your chest, say it. If it's work, then let's talk about it. Whatever it is, you need to either deal with it, or let the shit die. I'm not about to let you ruin my happiness because things are not about you."

"Not about me? When is it ever about me? You're the big-time business owner, Ms. College Degree with the nice bank account."

"Don't blame me because you made bad decisions in

your life. You had the same opportunities as me. You chose to do things differently."

"Same opportunities, my ass. I had to work when your prima-donna ass was hanging out at the mall."

"Prima donna? I think you've got me confused with someone else. Remember, I was the one who got you that job." I was up out of my seat by then. My temples were throbbing so hard I thought my head was going to explode. "You know what, Lonnie, anybody who doesn't cooperate with you, then the hell with them."

Lisa's phone was on the table near Cara. It started to ring. Cara picked it up and stared at the screen for a second. The look of shock on her face was cause for concern.

Lisa rushed over and grabbed the phone from her.

"Don't touch my shit! Damn!" She clicked the ignore button.

"Don't ignore it. Answer it, Lisa."

Lisa was working her way over to her purse; all the while still talking trash. "I don't have to answer nothing. You ain't have no business picking my phone up. Nosey bitch."

"What did you call me?"

"Nosey. That's what I said."

Ebonee was blocking her from getting her purse.

"Are you going to say something, or am I going to say it for you?"

Lisa gave Cara a threatening look.

"Lisa, why the hell is he calling you?" Cara's hands were planted firmly on her hips.

"Who?" Ebonee asked.

"I'll give you one more chance to explain yourself."

"Ebonee, could you move please?" Lisa continued to reach across Ebb for her purse.

Ebonee grabbed her hand and pushed her back.

"Damn, you need to back up."

"Lisa…" Cara stepped closer to her.

"What? Damn?"

"Why is Chauncey calling you?"

"Chauncey?" I looked at Cara and then back to Lisa. My breath was caught in my throat. I sat down to keep from falling.

"He's calling me. Why do I have to explain my business to you?"

"You know you crossed the line with that one?" Cara poked Lisa in the head.

"I know you better not touch me again."

"Or what? Your ass is so stupid. How could you do something like that to your friend?"

"'Cause she's not really her friend." Ebonee crossed her arms over her chest and looked at Lisa.

"I didn't see any of you saying anything when she talked to my exes."

"I really think your ass is delusional. Deeva has never talked to any boy, or man, after you've talked to him."

"Delusional? This bitch is bipolar. Talking stupid and

shit. Matter of fact, get out. Go call Chauncey back. I know it's killing you," Cara said.

As if on cue, her cell started to ring again.

"Who is Chauncey?" Lonnie leaned over and asked Ebonee.

"He's Deeva's old boyfriend. A boyfriend who did her really bad. So bad, we decided we wouldn't even say his name anymore. Remember that, Lisa?"

Lisa answered her phone. "Yeah. I'm coming. No, don't leave. I'm on my way down now."

"You got that niggah downstairs waiting for you?"

"Oh, hell no!" Ebonee jumped up and ran for the door.

I could hear the argument that was going on around me, but couldn't will myself to respond. The shock from hearing his name being used so freely, after more than two years, was causing a temporary loss of my motor skills—speech being the main one.

Cara glared at her. "You know what, Lisa? This is as low as you can stoop in the game of friendship."

"What gives you the right to judge me, Cara?"

"She's not the only one judging you. How could you do this to Deeva? As you so often like to remind anyone who will listen, you are her *oldest* friend."

"Been friends since kindergarten. Isn't that how she says it, Ebonee?"

Ebonee shook her head in disgust.

Lonnie put his hand on my shoulder.

"Deeva, are you okay?" All at once, everyone turned

and looked at me, as if the realization that I was still in the room had hit them.

Still unable to find my voice through the fog of bad memories that were flooding my brain, the most I could do was stand there in a stupor.

"You know what? I don't give a damn about what any of you think," Lisa said. "Just because he didn't love Deeva enough to do right by her—"

"What makes you so sure he won't do the same shit to you? What makes you think that what you're doing is any more or better than what I did? Yeah, he's downstairs now waiting for you. Probably rushing you to come on," I lashed out at her. "What you don't realize is that this is the only time he can get away. If you know like I know, you better get going." I stood up and went to the door and held it open for her.

"You know, Deeva, you try to act as if you're so righteous. Don't forget you haven't been completely honest with your man. I wonder what Tristan's going to think when he finds out the truth about you."

I calmly stepped close enough to her so there would be no mistaking my threat to her.

"I wouldn't worry about Tristan if I were you. Your hands will be full soon enough, when Chauncey's wife gets wind of this little secret rendezvous you're having. And don't fool yourself, thinking she's not going to find out. She always does."

"He's leaving her—"

"For you? Yeah, I heard the same thing after I discovered he had a wife. Difference is I didn't know he had one, but you do." I stepped back and resumed my position at the door.

She stepped across the threshold and turned to face me.

"I hope he was worth losing twenty-five years of friendship for."

She opened her mouth to respond, but I slammed the door in her face.

The silence in the room was deafening.

I could feel the tears I didn't want to shed building in my bottom lids. Tears for the loss of not only someone I considered a friend, but someone I considered to be my sister.

"Ya'll know you're going to have to tell me who in the hell this Chauncey character is and what the hell he did to my Deeva." Lonnie looked from me to Ebonee, and then Cara.

"Let's just say he was one of those annoying metal plates they use to cover the holes in the street, until someone decides to finally fix them."

CHAPTER 22

"I can't believe your girl would do something that slimy to you." Tristan rubbed his hands across my back.

We were relaxing in his room watching television, with me stretched out across his lap.

"I think we were all a bit surprised. It explains why she's been acting so irritable toward me."

"Damn, but to mess around with your ex? That's just shady."

He didn't know the half of it. Lisa had been right there with me when I'd gone through the nightmare of a relationship with Chauncey. Right there when his wife came knocking on my door—two kids in tow and one in her belly. Stood right next to me as the deranged woman produced a gun and promised to use it, if I didn't leave her husband alone. Lisa had been the one who insisted on being in the room with me after I made the decision to abort the fetus I'd been carrying for five months. A baby he and I had sat down and planned together. The baby I thought had been conceived through love with a man who had proposed marriage to me.

After learning all the lies Chauncey had told me, the

baby felt like another one. One I knew I wouldn't be able to stand to look at, or live with, for the rest of my life.

"What are you going to do about your bridesmaids? Should I tell one of the guys not to worry? Or do you have someone that'll take her place?"

For a moment, I thought about who I could ask.

"You know…" He paused and rubbed my back again. "You probably could ask Fallon to do it. You know, since Lorenzo is going to be my best man."

I sat up and looked at him.

"I thought Q was going to be your best man?"

"Q is not reliable enough. Plus, I'm closer friends with Lorenzo."

After the confrontation I'd had with Fallon a few weeks earlier, I didn't want to have to be in the same room with her. Let alone ask her to take part in my wedding.

"I think I'll ask my cousin," I said as I got up and walked into the bathroom.

"Baby, what have you got against Fallon?"

"Other than the fact that she's a bitch? Hmmm, let me see." I walked back into the room and joined him again on the bed. "Tristan, that woman still hopes there's a possibility you'll get with her girlfriend. She's already gotten two of you married off to her other girls. Besides, have you forgotten how rude she and her boyfriend were to me when I was a guest in their home?"

"Aww, baby." He pulled me over to him and kissed my face. "They know I don't want anyone but you."

"You know, I've been meaning to talk to you about something."

"What?" He wrapped his arms around me.

Before I could say another word, there was a knock at the door.

"Yeah?" Tristan yelled out.

"Daddy, can I come in?"

"Sure, T.J. Your dad and I are just watching TV." I sat up from my reclining position against Tristan's chest.

T.J. came in and climbed into the bed with us. I patted a space near me. He slid up to me and snuggled in.

"Hey, man. That's my spot."

"Tell him when you're not here it is. Other than that, this spot is yours exclusively." I hugged T.J. tight.

"You heard that, Dad?"

"Umm-hmm. I heard her." He pulled me back against his chest again.

"Deeva?"

"Yes, T.J."

"Since you said yes to our proposal, would you mind if I called you Mommy?"

I was so caught off guard. He had definitely grown on me and being his mother was one of the duties I was looking forward to doing.

"I would love for you to call me Mommy." The warm feel of heavy tears stung my eyes. I blinked them back as I leaned forward and kissed the top of his head.

Tristan kissed the side of my neck.

"This is perfect," he whispered in my ear.

I nodded my head in agreement. Things were perfect at this moment. Oh, but there was a storm brewing and headed my way.

CHAPTER 23

"Your parents are arriving at two o'clock today. I arranged to have a car pick them up, since you have your final fitting scheduled at noon." Lonnie continued to look at his PDA as he ran off the list of things to do.

"I can call the seamstress and see if she can change my appointment. Maybe go in a bit earlier. Then I can meet my parents at the airport."

"No. You'll do everything as planned so we can stay on schedule.

"Ms. Ebonee." He turned his attention to her. "As maid-of-honor your job is to make sure our bride gets to all of her appointments on time. Most importantly, you have to get her to the rehearsal dinner on time."

Ebonee grabbed her purse and gave Lonnie an officer's salute.

"Let's get going, bride. I don't want to mess around and end up on Ms. Lonnie's bad side."

"Is Cara coming with us?" I inquired.

"No, sweetie. Cara is in charge of the catering for tonight. She's already had her final fitting."

"Well, Ebonee. I guess it's just you and me today."

"I'm ready when you are."

I grabbed my purse and my bride planner bag Lonnie had given me.

"Are you getting nervous?"

"No. Not yet."

"What do you mean, not yet?"

"Nothing, girl. I'm not nervous though. Actually, I'm more excited than anything else. I'm ready to start my life as Mrs. Savage." I looked down at my engagement ring. Mindlessly, I fiddled with it. Turning it continuously.

"Have you been able to talk to him yet?" Ebonee turned onto the main highway headed for I-20.

"No."

"What are you waiting for, Deeva?"

"Every time I bring it up either the phone rings, someone knocks on the door, or he's busy with something else."

"You need to make him listen. You don't want—"

"I know, Ebonee. Damn, you're acting like I don't want to tell him. I have every intention of telling him before Saturday."

"Today is Thursday."

"I know, Ebonee."

"I'm not trying to get on your nerves. I want to make sure no one ruins your happiness. And while I don't think Tristan is going to be upset enough to call things off, I do think you should be the one to tell him."

"Okay. Okay. I'll tell him tonight when we get home."
I reached for the volume knob and turned up the radio.

"Don't get an attitude with me. I'm only doing my maid-of-honor duty."

I couldn't help but laugh.

"And you're doing a very good job of it."

CHAPTER 24

hankfully I'd purchased an outfit just for tonight or I know I would've been in the closet still looking for something to wear.

"Tristan called while you were in the bathroom."

"Why didn't you come and get me?"

"Uh, did I not just say you were in the bathroom?"

I ran and picked up my cell phone.

"How long ago did he call?" The phone was pressed between my left shoulder and ear as I put an earring in my other ear.

"Not too long ago."

His voicemail came on.

"Hey, baby. I was calling you back. I guess I'll see you when we get to the dinner. I love you. Bye." I snapped the phone shut. Looked in the mirror and finger-combed my hair into place.

"Have you talked to your mom and dad since they got here?"

"Yeah. They're going to meet us at the dinner. I thought Lonnie would've had them ride with me."

"You know Ms. Lonnie is a professional and a perfectionist. So, you know your parents are in good hands."

"You ready?" I turned and looked at Ebonee.

"Let's get going."

The pleated, tangerine halter dress exposed my bronze, toned shoulders in the late-evening sun. Legs for days seemed to extend from the bottom of the dress. Complemented with a strappy pair of three-quarter-inch, open-toed heels—the shoes were the icing on the cake.

I picked up my phone and dialed Tristan. Once again I got his voicemail.

"I wonder if he left yet." I put the cell back in my bag.

"He said he would meet us there."

"Okay." I looked out the window.

"Are you excited still?"

"Yes. My nerves are working overtime right now."

Ebonee smiled.

"It's only natural, girl. I was wondering when you were going to drop your cape."

"What you mean, drop my cape?"

"Girl, you always have to act like you're Super Chick or something. Like you can't let anything get to you."

"You know where that comes from. I've always had to take care of things so I tend to put my feelings aside."

"Well, tonight it's okay to be plain ol' Deeva."

"I'll remember that." I laughed.

We pulled into the driveway of what was clearly a mansion. A driveway so long that I knew they got their mail when they were either on their way out or in. We rode past a row of manicured Dogwood trees to the circular part of the driveway where we were greeted by Lonnie.

"Right on time." He looked down at his watch. "Everyone is around back by the pool." He hooked his arm through mine and led me into the house.

"Is Tristan here yet?"

"He's out back with everyone else."

"I wonder why he's not answering his phone."

We made our way through a large room with extremely high ceilings.

"Whose house is this?" Ebonee asked.

"A friend of mine. Her husband used to play professional football back in the day."

We walked out a set of glass doors to the deck area which was beautifully decorated with balloons and tiki torches that led down to the pool area.

"Oh, Lonnie, this is so nice!"

"I told you I was going to hook it up."

I searched through the crowd of people, looking for Tristan. Greeting guests along the way.

"There's my girl," my father said as he pulled me into an embrace. "You look beautiful." He held me away from him so he could have a better look.

"Hi, Daddy. Have you been here long?"

"About thirty minutes, but we got to meet our future son-in-law and his family about five minutes ago. Have you seen your mother yet?"

"Not yet."

"She's over there at the bar." He pointed to a corner on the other side of the pool.

"Figures," I mumbled under my breath.

"What was that?"

"Nothing. I'm going to say hello, since she's just getting started."

"Don't give her a hard time, Deeva."

"I'm not." I walked over to where my mother was holding court with the bartender and a male guest.

"Hello, Mother. I guess they have your brand tonight."

"Deeva." She barely moved her head before going back to her captive audience.

Usually I would go through the motions of trying to get her attention, but tonight was my night. I started walking away.

"Is that all you're going to say?"

"You seem to be a little preoccupied at the moment, so I'll talk to you later." I continued to walk back toward the house.

"Okay, everyone, we need to get this show on the road." I heard Lonnie's voice coming through the DJ's sound system.

"Deeva and Tristan, I need you to meet me out here by the pool."

I made my way back to the pool and stood next to Lonnie. I watched as Tristan emerged from a side door of the house. I smiled at him, but it was not reciprocated. His hands in his pockets, he stood next to me and looked at the guests as they joined us. I slid up next to him. The look he gave cut me deep and I knew this night was about to get worse.

Before I could get Lonnie's attention, his voice was once again coming through the microphone.

"What's wrong, Tristan?"

He shook his head from side to side; never saying a word. He walked over to Lonnie and asked if he could say a few words before we got started.

My heart was beating in my ears. I couldn't believe this was happening. I began to beat myself up verbally. *Why didn't you tell him?*

"Good evening, everyone. First, let me start by thanking each and every one of you for taking the time to come out and celebrate. Well, at least I thought this was going to be a celebration."

I could feel the mood shift as everyone got quiet so they could hear.

I rushed over to Tristan as gracefully as I could.

"Baby, let's go in the house and talk for a minute before you do this. Please?"

He looked at me, as if I disgusted him.

"If you ever loved me, you'll do this in private." I turned away from him and made a path through the crowd.

After standing his ground for a few seconds longer, he handed the microphone back to Lonnie and followed me.

Stunned, Lonnie looked at the mic in his hand and out at the crowd, who were watching us walk away. Lonnie looked at Ebonee and Cara for help.

"Just have the DJ play something. Get everyone to go

back to eating and drinking," Ebonee whispered in his ear. On her way through the crowd, she grabbed Cara's hand and followed the path Tristan and I had made.

Once inside the house, Tristan barely waited for the door to close good before he started.

"Damn, here I was thinking I'd found the woman of my dreams, and it was all a lie."

"No, Tristan. It's not what you think."

"It's not?"

"No."

"You're telling me Octavia didn't come to your office and pay you to spy on me? Talk to me, and see if I would fall for you?"

"She did, but—"

"But what? Damn, did you get a bonus for fucking me on the first date?"

"That's not fair."

"Not fair?! Don't even go there. What's not fair is an unsuspecting man thinking he's meeting a woman; not some girl who's into playing games."

"Tristan, I've been trying to tell you now—"

"Trying to tell me? Tell me what? The reason why you've never once told me you have your own business? Or was it the one about how you lied to me about working at an advertising firm? I guess you were too worried about me catching you out with another dude while you were *working*."

"Catch me out with someone?"

"That's how you do business, right? You go on a date,

or whatever it is. I can't believe I was stupid enough to think you were the one." He was talking through his teeth, which let me know he was seething with anger.

"Tristan, I am the one." I desperately grabbed at him. He yanked his arm away from me and looked at me as if I were a vile taste of something he had tried to swallow.

"Don't do this. Please. Not right now."

"Not right now? You think I'm going to go out there and fake like everything is okay? Make everyone think I'm going to marry someone who is a liar and a cheat? Bitch, get off me."

Shocked from the harshness of the word, I stepped back. In the seven months we'd been together, I'd never once heard him use such foul language. And especially not toward me.

I kept a slow pace as I backed away from him. Tears lined my cheeks.

"Deeva?" Ebonee asked as she placed her hand on my shoulder.

I was suddenly aware we weren't alone. All of his friends and mine were there. I spotted Lorenzo and Fallon standing in a corner near the door. I slowly made my way over to them.

"I hope you're both happy. Sad thing about it is while your story may have some truth to it, it didn't happen quite the way you think, but I don't have to explain to anyone."

I continued out the door, with Ebonee and Cara on my heels.

"Deeva! Deeva, slow down and wait a minute."

I didn't stop until I was outside. I desperately searched for my car, only to remember I rode with Ebonee. Frustrated, I started down the driveway past the gawking latecomers who were trying to figure out why the intended bride was leaving in such a rush.

"Deeva!" Cara and Ebonee shouted.

I could hear the sound of a car's engine getting closer to me.

Just keep walking until no one can see you.

The car was getting nearer as I got closer to being back on the street and out of the long winding driveway.

"Deeva, I know you hear me. Get in." Ebonee and Cara pulled up beside me. Cara got out and led me to the car.

I quickly slid into the backseat.

"Your house or mine?"

"Yours is closer," Cara reminded Ebonee.

Not another word was said during the short five-mile ride to her house.

As soon as I put my foot in her front door, a deep, wrenching sob escaped from me. I sank to the floor.

"Come on, Deeva. Let's go to my room." Ebonee signaled for Cara to grab me from the other side.

"It'll be okay."

"No! No, it won't be okay. I tried to tell him. I swear I tried." I sobbed.

"We know. We know." Ebonee pulled back the cover on her king-sized bed.

"Give him time, Dee. He's going to need some time."

"Cara, I don't think there'll ever be enough time to help him get over the hurt, humiliation, and betrayal he's feeling. He thinks I betrayed him. He actually thinks I go out and get with other men."

I curled up in a fetal position. What is it about the position that makes you feel like you are protected from anything that can ever hurt you? Pulling your legs into your chest, wrapping your arms around your legs, and holding your body tightly.

I began a slow rock. I had been there before. A slow shutdown of your feelings as your thoughts damn near drive you insane. Once again being comforted by my friends. At least, the ones who mattered the most.

"Get some rest. We're going to go back over and let Lonnie and your parents know what's going on."

My parents. I hadn't thought about them until that moment. I knew my mom would get a real thrill out of this. A disappointment once again. She didn't care what I did, as long as it didn't come back on her.

I could hear the front door close. As a diversion, Ebonee had turned the TV on to keep me company. I didn't have the strength to lift my head, let alone focus on what was happening on the screen.

My heart was hurting and this time it was my fault. There was nowhere to lay the blame but at my feet. I'd had chance after chance to tell him, but once again, I had let someone else control my fate. Something I had promised myself to never let happen again.

CHAPTER 25

I was startled awake by the sound of a ringing phone. The darkness of the room seemed to envelop me in a tight but soothing grasp. I lay there silent and still. Listening for any other signs that would let me know I wasn't still alone.

The weight of my eyelids, evidence of the earlier non-stop crying session, let me know I was going to find a swollen, puffy mess when I looked into a mirror.

"She's still sleeping," I could hear Ebonee explaining to someone. "Yeah. I know, but he was pretty brutal. Oh, you know I let his ass know it, too." There was a pause in her words. I could tell she was on the phone, listening to the other person talk. "Well, he should've been man enough to call her or at least waited until they were alone. The whole humiliation thing, that shit was dead-ass wrong."

Silence again.

"I couldn't believe he was still there when we got back. Why the fuck didn't he leave?"

"Didn't you say you were trying to stop cursing?" I heard Cara say.

"I did, but this shit has me thirty-eight hot."

I slowly raised my head so I could sit in an upright position. A wave of emptiness passed through me, but I had to get up.

"This is going to take some real sistah-girl intervention. So ya'll get ready."

Still moving at a snail's pace, I stood up. I glanced around the room and turned in the direction of the bathroom. The hollow feeling was getting stronger. I was going to have to hurry up and get to the bathroom before I made a mess on Ebonee's floor.

After a ten-minute session of dry heaves, I washed my face and stared in the mirror for a second. The hollow-set eyes and smeared makeup were a pitiful sight. I took a few deep breaths before I was ready to face my friends. I had hidden out for the past few hours and that was long enough. I entered the kitchen where Ebonee and Cara were sitting at the breakfast bar.

"I know. I look like shit and feel like hell, but can I get something to eat?" I stood in the doorway to the kitchen in my crumpled dress and bare feet.

Cara jumped up and came over to me and wrapped her arms around me.

"It's going to be okay." She patted my back as she led me over to the barstool at the counter to have a seat.

"Nasha, let me call you back. She just got up. Okay. I'll let you know. Bye." Ebonee went into the fridge and rummaged around for a couple of seconds. She emerged with the items for a quick salad. She looked at me for approval.

"A small one will be good."

"I know it may feel like the end of the world right now, but you're a fighter and we know you'll get through this."

"Not only will she get through this, she'll come out on top." Ebonee opened the drawer and retrieved a knife.

"How did my parents take the news?" I took a seat and watched Ebonee as she sliced and diced everything up.

"Of course, your dad was worried about you. I told him I'd have you call him."

"And my mother?"

They both looked at each other and then back at me.

"You know our friendship is built on honesty."

Cara took a deep breath and slid into the chair next to me.

"You know your mom is in a class by herself."

"That I do know. So, was she sober enough to understand what was going on?"

"Deeva, you need to talk with your mom. She hasn't been right since—"

"He was my brother and my father's son, but neither one of us has cracked up behind it."

"But he was a mama's boy. Their relationship—"

I put my hand up. I'd heard enough.

"I have enough to deal with as is." I buried my face in my hand.

I had to figure out what I was going to do next. If I

could've gone back in time, I would've started at the beginning of the week. I would've sat Tristan down and told him everything, but time travel wasn't possible.

"Did Tristan leave when I left?"

Ebonee took a deep breath this time.

"Let's not talk about that now. Here." She placed the bowl of salad in front of me.

"How can I not talk about it?" I stared at the salad before picking up the fork and doing my best to eat as much of it as I could.

"Well, I'm down to do whatever you want. We can do a ride-through if you want."

"Cara!"

"What?"

I started to laugh and, once again, we were in high school. Riding by someone's man's house to see if he was home like he said and, if he was, was he alone. Ready to throw down, if it the moment called for it.

"I'm serious, Deeva. I understand he's hurt because he feels like you lied and trapped him or something, but all that shit he was talking today, I'm ready to check his ass for real."

"What shit?"

"Don't listen to her. You're going to be a lady about this and when it's all said and done, he's going to be the one who looks like shit in the end."

"Ebonee, what happened after I left?"

"I'll tell you what happened."

"Cara!"

"He didn't come out where everybody was, but he definitely said a mouthful to those who were in the basement with him. And that bitch Fallon, I was about to snatch her ass up for real."

"What did she have to say?"

"She was in the middle of everything. Telling Tristan how she never trusted you. How he should've stuck with Octavia. Octavia would've never done anything like this to him. Then the bitch wanted to start talking about how she should let people know what kind of business practices you have. Let them know how you ended up dating one of the people you were investigating. See if people would use your company then."

"She what?!"

"Girl, she didn't know I worked with you. So, you know I politely told her if she did anything remotely close to what she was talking about, she would regret the day she ever thought about you."

"You know she didn't say it quite as nice as that." Ebonee gave me a knowing glance. "Now, I have to admit. That shit there was funny. She must've turned three shades lighter by the time Cara was finished with her." Ebonee laughed loudly.

I chuckled a little. "Wish I could've been there to see it."

"Huh, I shut all their asses up. Tristan included."

The mention of him bad-mouthing me stabbed at my heart. I pushed the plate away; after only eating half of it. I noticed the look on Ebonee's face. She was in mothering mode and I knew she was going to be there until she felt I was in a better place.

"Where's my purse?"

"In my room."

I got up and walked back into her room and found my purse on the chaise. The vibrating of the cell phone I was searching for made me rush so I wouldn't miss the call. On the screen was a local number, but one that wasn't programmed into my phone.

"Hello?"

"Deeva? It's Daddy. I was just checking on you."

"Hey, Daddy."

"Are you okay?"

"I guess I'll survive."

"You're a McCoy. We always bounce back. Believe me, baby, he'll come around."

"Are you sure, Daddy?"

"You know men can be pig-headed sometimes. We jump to conclusions and make mistakes. Once he figures out you're the best thing to ever happen to him, he'll be calling."

"Thanks, Daddy. You always know how to make me feel better."

"That's what daddies do."

We talked a few minutes longer. He promised to come see me the next day. While I was excited to see him, I wished he would leave my mom at the hotel.

I went through my recent call list to see if Tristan had tried to call me while I was sleeping. Not a call from him since the one earlier in the day.

Ebonee was finishing the last of the salad on my plate.

"You know I'm not going to let good food go to waste."

"I ain't mad at you."

"Did he call?"

"No."

"So what are we going to do?" Cara picked a piece of cucumber off the plate.

"I think it's time to get even." I flipped open my phone and called Lonnie.

CHAPTER 26

"Man, you look like shit."

"I'm glad to see you, too, Q." Tristan held the door open and Quincy walked in.

"Have you called to apologize to her yet?"

"Man, don't come in here with that shit. I'm not in the mood."

Quincy sat on the sofa and grabbed the remote from the table.

"You know you were wrong the way you handled things."

Tristan joined him on the sofa and snatched the remote from him.

"This coming from a man who prides himself on dogging women."

"The women I deal with are nowhere near as classy as Deeva. You can't compare apples to oranges."

Tristan increased the volume on the television.

"Look, Deeva wasn't straightforward with me."

"Straightforward? Have you forgotten you *were* messing around with Octavia when you spent the weekend with her?"

"I wasn't serious with Octavia. Besides, Deeva knew the deal. She was the one who initiated the sex that weekend."

"Okay. If that's what you want to believe."

"Why are you so pro Deeva? Do you not understand what she did?"

"What did she do that was so bad? If you ask me, she sounds like a very smart woman with a very successful business. Did she pressure you into anything? I don't remember you telling me anything about her holding a gun to your head."

"Q, man, she tricked me into thinking our meeting was a random act. I bet the argument she was having with her friend that night was staged. "

"You talking about the one she isn't speaking to because she crossed her and started messing with her ex? Better yet, the one who crossed her and called and gave you the information you're tripping on? Yeah, I can imagine that argument being staged."

Tristan began to think about the phone call he'd gotten the morning of the rehearsal dinner. He was curious as to why Lisa was calling him. Thinking she wanted him to intervene and talk to Deeva so she would let her come to the wedding, he called her back. What he got instead was unexpected and, in the end, devastating.

"That chick has some real issues. I don't see how Deeva ever considered her to be a friend at all. I don't care how mad we get, I'll never do the underhanded shit she did to any of you. Not even to Lorenzo, and you know how I feel about his pussy-whipped ass."

Tristan laughed.

"Leave Lorenzo alone."

"Man, fuck Lorenzo and his busybody bitch of a girl, Fallon. You know Fallon probably pushed Octavia up to having you investigated in the first place."

He could be right, Tristan thought.

"I don't know, Tristan. I really think you need to rethink this before you fuck around and lose the best thing to ever happen to you."

"How do you think she's the best thing to ever happen to me?"

"How many women have you asked to marry you?"

Tristan sat and thought for a minute.

"Umm-hmm. Now, if she was good enough for you to pop the question to, why does one misdeed make her so bad? Even T.J. is in love with her. Hell, I'm in love with her."

"I'm starting to notice."

"Whatever, niggah. You know what I mean."

"I know, but you have to also understand how betrayed I feel. You're not only my boy, but you're also a man. So, tell me how would you feel if you found out the woman you were about to marry was spying on you?"

"Shit, man, it would be a normal occurrence for me. I mean, if I'm about to marry a chick, she better make sure I have all these doggish ways out of my system."

"Niggah, can you be serious for one minute?" Tristan tossed a pillow at Quincy's head.

"I am being serious."

They both laughed for a minute. Once the laughing was done, they sat quietly staring at the television screen.

"Look, Deeva is a real jewel, Tristan. Maybe there's more to this story than you've been told. I understand right now you don't want to talk to Deeva, but maybe you should talk to some other people who may have a few answers you need right now."

"Who?"

"Octavia, for one. Plus, I'm getting a feeling Lorenzo and Fallon know more than they're telling."

Tristan sat and thought about his options. Lorenzo and Fallon had never really taken to him being with Deeva. Maybe they had a reason as to why.

"A few days ago, you told me this woman was your reason for breathing. Now, I've never had a feeling that deep for a woman in my life but once, and that was my mama. If you loved her that much a few days ago, you should still have the same feelings for her now. Loving a woman that deep is hard to give up just like that." He snapped his fingers.

Tristan trailed his hands down his face and took a deep breath. He ran his hand back up to his head and rubbed it vigorously.

"Daddy?"

Tristan turned to see T.J. standing at the end of the stairs.

"Yeah?"

"Is Deeva coming over tomorrow? She's supposed to help me with my class project."

He saw a familiar look in his son's eyes. The same look he would get when he asked about his mother. T.J. was worried Deeva would abandon him the same way his mom had, but was scared to tell his dad.

"I think she's going to be busy tomorrow, but I can help you."

T.J. dropped his head and turned to go back up the stairs.

"That's okay. She's the only one who can help me. I'll wait until she can come."

Quincy shook his head as he looked at Tristan. "And you want to put this boy through this again? You better make sure you're making the right decision."

CHAPTER 27

I turned on my computer for the first time in four days. Before I had logged on good, my calendar popped open and showed the appointments I had missed during my time of mourning.

"T.J.," I said softly. I looked at the time of the appointment and then checked the time on my computer. If I rushed, I would get there before it was too late. Should I go? Maybe I need to make a clean break from him. But he's depending on me so I have to go.

I jumped up and ran into my room to get ready. T.J. had had enough letdowns in his life from his mother and since he thought of me in the same capacity, I wasn't about to let him down and have him think all women would be a letdown to him. I would give up Tristan. Go cold turkey until it didn't hurt so bad to love him. But T.J. I was going to hold onto T.J. until someone pried my fingers off of him.

"Deeva!" T.J. ran over to me and wrapped his arms around my neck.

I was glad to see Tristan hadn't taken me off the list of people able to come to the school for him.

"Hey, baby. How are you?" I hugged him tightly.

"I'm okay. I really miss you, Deeva."

"Oh, T.J., I miss you, too."

"Deeva, are you still going to marry my daddy? Are you still going to be my mommy?"

Stunned by the bluntness of his questions, I didn't know what to tell him. I stared into his expectant face. The pure innocence of him caused tears to well in the bottom of my eyes.

"Daddy and I need a little time to figure some things out. You know I'll always be here for you, no matter what. Okay?"

He shook his head.

"Are you ready to go?"

"Yep. I have some of the things we're going to need in my book bag." He patted the huge bag on his back.

"Well, let's get going so we can get you home at a decent hour." I tweaked his nose, then grabbed his hand.

I'd called and let Tristan's mom know I was going to pick T.J. up so she wouldn't have to come get him. She was glad to hear from me and told me she'd let Tristan know T.J. was with me.

I took him to the library so we could get the different books we would need for our research.

"Are you sure you're in the fifth grade?" I asked as I stared at the mountain of books in front of us.

"Of course, Deeva. You know I am." He laughed.

"When I was in fifth grade, we didn't have this much work to do."

"Well, I wish I went to school back in the old days then."

"The old days? Are you calling me old?"

"You are old, Deeva." He laughed again.

"Okay, we're going to quit while we're ahead. You're starting to hurt my feelings." I faked as if I was going to cry.

T.J. kissed my cheek and grabbed the first book off the pile.

We spent the next three hours taking notes and mapping out the pages and outlines he needed. Our table was full of papers and markers we were using to make sure his project looked nice and creative.

"So, what do you think?"

He held the report up and handed it to me. I slowly flipped through each page, making sure everything was as perfect as we could make it.

"I think you're going to get an A for this." I handed it back to him and started cleaning everything up.

"Are you taking me to Grandma's house?" He put his supplies back into his book bag.

"Isn't your dad going to pick you up from there?"

He shrugged his shoulders.

We put all the books we had taken out on the book cart near the desk and headed downstairs to the exit.

"I just had a great idea!"

"And what would that be?"

"We could stop and get something to eat at CiCi's Pizza."

"I think I can handle that." I unlocked the car doors and watched him as he climbed into the front seat next to me.

"I was also thinking we could call my daddy and see if he would meet us there."

While I wanted nothing more than to be one happy family again with Tristan and T.J., I knew Tristan wasn't going to have any part of it.

"Maybe another time?"

I saw his shoulders slump a little.

"Do you still want to go with just me?"

He shook his head yes and looked out the window.

"I still want you to be my mommy, Deeva."

"And I still want to be, sweetie. Look, sometimes grown-ups do really stupid things, but we eventually figure it out."

"I hope you guys figure it out soon."

CHAPTER 28

"Daddy, how long are you going to be mad at Deeva?"

Tristan looked a bit caught off guard as he pulled the cover back for T.J. to get into bed.

"Who said anything about me being mad with Deeva?"

"I heard you and Uncle Q talking. Plus Grandma was talking to Auntie Thomasina about it." T.J. climbed into his bed and lay down.

"You're listening to grownup talk. Right now, it's hard to explain to you what's going on with me and Deeva."

"Do you love her?"

"Where is all this questioning coming from?"

"Nowhere. I was just wondering, is all."

Tristan pulled the covers up to T.J.'s chin.

"You let your dad here handle the situation with Deeva. Regardless of what happens, you and I will be fine."

T.J. looked at Tristan, then sighed.

"Good night, Dad." He rolled over on his side.

"Good night, son," Tristan said to T.J.'s back and slowly closed the door.

His mom told him Deeva had kept her word about

helping T.J. with his school project. Once she gave him all the details of T.J.'s outing with Deeva, she then commenced to tell him how much of a fool he was for continuing to deal with the problem with Deeva as if he were some immature high school boy.

"And if you don't believe me, go ask your father." She placed the oven mitt on the counter and walked into the room where her husband was watching television.

Tristan was not in the mood for a lecture, but knew there was no getting around it. Reluctantly, he got up from his seat at the table and followed. He stood in the doorway for a minute before his dad even looked up.

"Your mother is right, but you're a grown man and have been making your own choices for years now. So, it's on you how you handle this."

Not extremely satisfied with her husband's choice of words, Tristan's mother looked at him, shook her head, and walked out of the room.

"I appreciate that, Pops."

"Umm-hmm. Now I have to go upstairs and convince your mama this is none of our business and hope she lets me sleep in my bed tonight."

"I'm not here to start any problems. I came by to pick my son up."

"Yeah, well, a word of advice."

Tristan had started to climb the stairs and stopped.

"A woman will mourn the loss of a relationship, but she'll only mourn for so long. Just like a cut, all things start to heal. Now, it's up to you whether or not you'll heal together. And as much as I hate to be in your business, son, I really think you should talk with her so you can go through the healing process together. If I could've, would've, should've are hard pills to swallow."

With that, Mr. Savage turned the television back up. His attention was once again on his favorite program.

Tristan slowly climbed the stairs as he focused on the words of his father. He'd gone through the regret game with Priscilla. He'd blamed himself for her drug addiction in the beginning. If only he would've done this or he could've done that she would've been okay. But, in time, he realized she had her own demons she was dealing with and the drugs were merely an escape. While temporary, they were what she thought she needed to get rid of them.

He walked into his old bedroom where T.J. was sound asleep. He went over to the desk to gather his things and noticed the nicely decorated folder. He picked it up and flipped through it. T.J. was sure to get an A for this project. It was nothing like the ones he'd helped him with in the past.

He looked at his son lying on the bottom bunk. His innocence was endearing.

"He told her he still wants her to be his mother."

"Yeah, he's told me the same thing." Tristan placed the report in T.J.'s backpack.

"I told you when you first brought her home, she was your soul mate. I felt it then and I feel it now."

"Mama, I—"

"Listen, I'm going to take your father's advice and let

you make your *own* decision. But I'm your mama and I love you. It's hard for me to stand by and watch you make a mistake."

"Why is everyone so sure I'm making a mistake, if I decide to leave Deeva alone? Has anyone thought about how her actions hurt me? How I might be humiliated by them?"

"Let's see, she announced to the world she met you because someone came to her company to have you investigated, but somewhere along the way she decided to start dating you and then accepted your marriage proposal. Hmm, I seem to remember you being the one to do that. I believe it happened how Deeva said. Or have you talked to her to find out her side of the story?" She gave Tristan a challenging look and he looked away. "I didn't think so."

Mrs. Savage walked over and kissed her son on the cheek.

"I love you, baby. I guess that's all that matters." She patted his shoulder and then walked out of the room.

Tristan placed T.J.'s backpack on his arm and then picked the sleeping child up.

"You're getting heavy, lil' man." He threw him up on his shoulder

"Okay, Pops. I'll catch you later," Tristan called to his father as he reached the bottom of the stairs.

"Alright, son." Mr. Savage threw his hand up without glancing away from the TV.

He looked at T.J. who was securely tucked in.

He'd thought about what his parents had said all the way home that night. Had he been brash in his decision to write off Deeva? Maybe, but everyone had to understand his pain. He'd explained to her from the beginning that he didn't ask her for anything except for her honesty. How could she be honest when the whole relationship was a lie? He'd already had a relationship built on lies and he wasn't going through that again. The question from his parents was still in the air though. Had he given Deeva a fair chance to explain? No, he hadn't thought to give Deeva a chance to explain or better yet, lie her way out of the situation. What could she say to make things better?

"Maybe I'll call her later this week," Tristan said aloud as he pulled T.J.'s room door in. "I would love to hear what she has to say."

CHAPTER 29

"Lonnie, I've been meaning to ask you about the information I asked you to check into a few months back."

"I was wondering when you were going to ask me about it." Lonnie walked out of my office and returned with a folder. He slid it over to me as he sat back down in the chair in front of my desk. "Here."

I slowly browsed through the contents. "Well, I'll be damned."

"Umm-hmm."

"How did you get this?"

"Girl, what's my name? I had to go way back and do some deep, deep digging."

"No wonder he hasn't married her." I continued to look, with my mouth propped open. Adding a headshake every now and then.

"Now you have all the ammunition you need."

Lonnie was right. If revenge was what I was seeking, then this information here would blow them off the map. I placed the folder in the bottom drawer of my desk.

"Aren't you going to use it?"

"Of course, she is. That bitch Fallon needs to be brought down a couple of notches. Her and her *man*." Cara and Lonnie slapped hands and laughed.

On the other hand, I was unsure whether or not I was going to use the information or not. People had gotten killed behind stuff like this. While I was definitely upset they had gone to Tristan and sabotaged my happiness—our happiness—I had never done anything as malicious as this in my life.

"I'll keep it in here, for just-in-case causes." I closed the drawer.

The lively chatter between the two stopped as they both turned and looked at me as if I had instantly grown another head.

"Just in case what? Need I remind you of the wedding that was supposed to happen a month ago but didn't because of them?"

"Cara, I have to deal with this in my own way. I've been talking to someone and—"

"You're seeing a shrink?"

"Did I say I was in therapy?"

"No, but that's usually what talking to someone is."

"No, Lonnie, talking to someone means I have someone I talk to about what's going on with me."

"Who, then?"

I knew they were going to question me from the moment I slipped and mentioned it.

"What?"

"If you're not talking to a therapist and you're definitely not talking to one of us, then who are you talking to?" Cara crossed her arms over her chest and sat back in the chair. Lonnie followed suit.

"Let's just say a friend."

"A friend?"

"Bitch, are you cheating on Tristan?!" Lonnie jumped up from his chair, almost knocking it over.

"No. Nothing like that."

"Then what is it like?"

I blew out a chest full of air and slowly rolled my neck in a circular motion before sitting back in my chair. "I've been talking to Q, okay?"

"Q?" Lonnie looked at me and then Cara, whose mouth was wide open.

"His friend, Deeva?"

"His friend? Whose friend?" Lonnie asked.

"It's not like that, Cara. He called me to make sure I was okay and to reassure me things would work out. He lets me know how Tristan is doing."

"Why not call Tristan and ask *him* how he's doing?"

"Because when I tried to call him, he didn't answer."

The room went silent for a moment.

"But his friend, Deeva? That's a bad move."

"What makes you so sure, Cara?"

"Lisa claims Chauncey called her to make sure you were okay."

That comment was like getting hit by a brick upside

the head. I really had no interest in Quincy and I doubted very seriously if he was interested in me. Even though I hadn't talked to Tristan in more than a month, I was still very much in love with him and from the information I was getting from Q, he hadn't completely written me off.

"Well, I'm not Lisa." I got up from my desk and walked over to the window. The cars on the street were starting to swell, as it was the end of the workday for most people. I watched as pedestrians seemed to rush from one place to another.

"Look, Deeva, I'm not trying to give you a hard time, but I know how much you love Tristan. I know talking to his friend seems harmless, but what if Quincy develops feelings for you? Then what? And don't say it can't happen, because it happens all the time."

I continued to gaze out the window as I thought about how Quincy had made an effort to reassure me things were going to be okay between Tristan and me. Tristan needed time to get over the hard feelings he'd developed from hearing what seemed to be, at the time, a non-trust issue.

"Deeva, you've let more than enough time go. I think you need to call him. If he still can't see beyond the incident, then move on. Always remember, it's his loss."

His loss. His loss. I'd been hearing those words quite often lately. If it was his loss, why was I the one feeling as if I was on the losing end?

CHAPTER 30

Tristan had decided it was time for him to try and make an effort to move forward. Even though he hadn't made any attempt to contact Deeva, as of yet, he knew he would have to in order to sort out his feelings.

Still slightly angry with her, he took his boys up on their offer to go out for a night of fun. Maybe he needed to dance and drink a little, in an effort to clear up some mental chaos going on in his head.

"I can't believe you still haven't called her," Quincy chided. "Believe it or not, she's hurting, too."

"And how would you know?"

Lorenzo glared at Quincy. "'Cause he's been calling your girl on a regular."

"Only to tell her to hang in there," Quincy replied. "Eventually you'll come to your senses. Don't listen to that bitter-ass niggah over there." He shot Lorenzo a warning glance.

"Why does he have to be the one to come to his senses? Tristan, man, has she tried to contact you?"

Tristan looked at Lorenzo and Quincy. In the beginning, she would call and leave him a short message every day. After a few weeks of unreturned calls, those messages began to come less and less, until they stopped altogether. Then, for a while, he was able to get tidbits of information about her through his mom and T.J., but even their comments had become few and far between, since she'd started to come around less.

Lorenzo said, "Make her ass come to you. She's the one who owes you an apology."

"If you ask me, you owe him one, too," Quincy said. "You knew about Octavia going to her in the first place, didn't you?"

"Man, I ain't know shit. So stop saying that bullshit." Lorenzo's voice was laced with anger. He stared Quincy down, more so as a threat than anything else.

"If Fallon knew, your ass knew."

"Motherfucker, I told you—"

"Alright! Enough!" Tristan stepped in to keep them apart. "It doesn't matter whether he knew or not. Whatever happens from this point forward is on me. Right now, what I want to happen is for us to leave and get to the club at a decent time so I can enjoy myself." He looked from one to the other.

"I'll meet ya'll there," Quincy said as he backed away, all the while staring at Lorenzo with as much disgust as he could muster up.

"Alright. We'll see you later then."

"You ready, Lorenzo? Jackson and Delante should be there and Fred and Malik said they'd be there later."

Lorenzo grabbed his cell phone from the table along with his keys.

"I'll drive. I might leave a little early, but you can catch a ride with one of the other guys."

Tristan shrugged his shoulders. "Cool."

The atmosphere of the club was on high. The music was bumping loudly from every corner of the room. Bodies were back to back on the dance floor. Everyone was gyrating to the uptempo dance tune.

Tristan, himself one of the bodies, was oblivious to everything around him as he enjoyed a stimulating, sexually charged dance from a woman he'd seen in passing a few times. The positioning and close proximity of their bodies could easily be mistaken for a sexual act. The redbone, with the short natural hair, dyed a bright blonde color, was grinding her ass back into his dick. The positioning of his hand at her hip as he held onto her added to the scene. Occasionally running his hand underneath the black "freekum" dress that hugged her body in all the right places, he had discovered a panty-less treasure. The more he rubbed, the harder she would grind back into him. Cloaked underneath darkness, Tristan took full advantage of the situation as he slid his hand toward her front; over and between her thighs. She leaned back and moaned in his ear. A clear indication she was willing to let this dance be what it was headed to being. Assured he could move forward, he slowly parted the lips of her pussy and slid his finger back and forth. Their dancing had taken on a whole new rhythm as he found her clit and put pressure on it with one finger while inserting another one inside her.

Deeva walked into the club accompanied by her trusted crew—Ebonee, Cara, and Lonnie. She looked around to see if she saw Quincy, who had been the one to suggest they come to the club tonight. She was hesitant at first, but gave in when Cara wouldn't let it go.

"Girl, I'm glad you decided to come. I know you were planning on resting, but you've been doing enough of that lately. You need to let your hair down tonight and have a little fun," said Cara as she got into a semi-squat and popped her butt in and out to the rhythm.

Deeva laughed. "Alright now, don't hurt yourself."

"Shoot, you mean don't hurt anybody else," Lonnie said as he backed away from her.

Deeva scanned the room. "I see a table over there." She pointed in the direction of the bar near the dance floor.

"We didn't come here to post up at a table. Come on." Cara pulled her and Ebonee onto the dance floor. "Come on, Lonnie."

"No, you girls get it started while I get a lil' something to quench my thirst." He placed his hand delicately on his throat and walked toward the bar as the girls slipped deeper into the crowd.

"Heeeyyy!" Cara threw her hands up as the beginning riffs of her favorite song wafted in on the outgoing beats of the song that was playing.

"Work it, Beyonce's cousin!" Ebonee hollered.

They danced together in the sacred "girls only" circle. The circle most guys were reluctant to break unless invited.

"Damn, is homeboy fucking her?" Deeva heard from behind her.

Boy, the things people will do in a club, she thought as she continued to dance.

"I think he is," a second voice chimed in, filled with a hint of excitement.

Curiosity being what it is, Deeva decided to be voyeuristic. She slowly turned until her back was toward Ebonee and Cara. The body belonging to the voice behind her had moved, offering her a clear view of the suspected couple.

"Oh my God," she said underneath her breath.

The positioning and motion of the arm thrust toward the front of the woman was a clear indication his fingers were at work.

Deeva turned her head to get Ebonee's and Cara's attention.

"Do ya'll see this?" She motioned with her head, toward what she was talking about.

"Dayum! Are they fucking?" Cara leaned in to ask.

"It sure looks like it." Deeva continued to look, even though she didn't want to seem too obvious.

Oblivious to the audience that was starting to gather, the sex dance continued until a few moments later when his dance partner reached her peak. With slippery wet fingers as evidence of the deed, Tristan seemed to come out of a thick fog. After allowing her enough time to gather her strength where she could stand on her own, he stepped back from his dance partner and looked to find approving smiles from a couple of guys who were close enough to know what was going on. They parted a small path. One even patted him on the back as he passed by. When he reached the end of the path, he looked up into a pair of familiar eyes. Eyes filled with shock and hurt; more profound with the sight of brimming tears.

"Deeva," he whispered as he reached out for her.

Hurt and humiliated, Deeva backed away as if his very touch would burn her.

Standing behind her, Cara and Ebonee embraced her as they shot killer looks toward Tristan.

"Don't you think you should wash your hands first?" Cara asked as Ebonee parted the crowd, leading Deeva toward the exit.

"Cara..., I..., I..."

Cara looked him up and down. "You don't have to say nothing. I can tell by just looking at you, how sorry you are." She shook her head. "And to think, she has been depressed about you."

Tristan watched as Cara walked away from him. Now

every bad thing he'd thought about what Deeva had done to him didn't matter. The look on her face let him know his actions had hurt her far worse. He slowly walked back over to where his boys were waiting on him. The expression on their faces let him know they had witnessed everything; more than likely from start to finish.

"You really should go wash your hands," Quincy said as he pushed past him.

Tristan glanced down at his hands. What had he been thinking? Performing a random sex act in public? He'd gotten caught up in a feeling. He realized all the while he was dancing with the other girl, it was Deeva he was thinking of. Deeva's softness. Deeva's sweet smell. It had taken him a month to know how much he missed her, but the realization he had probably done more damage tonight than could be repaired slapped him in the face. At least he thought it was slapping him, until he felt another sharp sting on his face. This one followed by words.

"You, nasty bastard! How could you do this to me?!" She smacked him again as Ebonee and Cara rushed behind her, trying to grab her before she could strike him again.

Tristan raised his hands to protect himself. "Deeva, baby, wait."

"Baby?! Now I'm your baby?!"

Everyone in the club gravitated over toward the action.

"Deeva, this isn't the time or place for this," Ebonee said as she grabbed ahold of her elbow.

"I hate you! I hate the day I met you! I especially hate that I didn't leave your ass alone after that bitch came to my office asking me to investigate you!"

"Deeva, let's go."

She looked at Ebonee as if it were the first time she noticed she was standing there. No longer able to control her emotions, Deeva broke down and began to cry.

Tristan's insides seemed to instantly hollow out. He reached out for Deeva.

"I got her," Ebonee assured him. She slowly positioned her arm around Deeva so she could guide her out. As she turned around, she was met by security.

"We're leaving," Ebonee informed him.

The burly bouncer looked over to Tristan. "I have to ask all of you to leave."

Tristan nodded and slowly began to walk out following behind Deeva and Ebonee, who were now being helped by another member of the security staff.

Cara and Lonnie were waiting with the car when they all got outside.

Tristan watched helplessly as Deeva was placed into the car. She looked over at him one last time. Tears streaming down her face, she glared at him until the car was out of sight.

Tristan sank down on the curb. How had this night gone so wrong? He was only going out for a little bit of fun. A night out with the boys. As he sat there pondering his situation, the blonde he'd been dancing with earlier walked by.

"Sorry about the mess, but it's evident homegirl isn't doing something right. So, here…" She grabbed his hand and placed a card firmly in his palm. "Give me a call, if you'd like to finish what we started." She closed his fingers around the card, winked, and walked away.

Tristan looked down at it and let it fall from his hand. The same hand that earlier had been between her legs.

How long had Deeva been standing there watching? The thought of the hurt he saw in Deeva's eyes made his heart sink. He realized how wrong he'd been for the way he had handled things between them before. Now he wondered if he would ever be able to make it right.

CHAPTER 31

I hadn't been into the office for almost two weeks. The depression I'd been fighting so hard against for a month had all but consumed me. I hadn't answered any phone calls. Hadn't looked at any emails. I had pretty much cut myself off from the real world. Eventually, I was going to have to rejoin it, but at the present moment, I wasn't interested.

Both Ebonee and Cara had called. Each one leaving a message about how they knew I was going to need time to get through this, and they were both available when I was ready to talk. My girls always had my back, but I was going to take the time they were giving me. They both had a key to get in and it wouldn't be long before one of them decided to use one.

Then, there were the calls from Quincy. His concern was evident in his voice. He apologized for inviting me out to the club that night. He never thought it would've turned out the way it did. He was only hoping once Tristan saw me, it would've triggered something and made him see how much he missed me.

Yeah, he missed me alright.

I slinked my way into the kitchen; dragging my feet as I went along. Clad in an oversized T-shirt and pair of boxers Tristan had left there, I was definitely dressed for the part of a severely depressed person. I reached for the box of cereal I had been snacking on all day. Not that it was a preference, but it was the only thing I was able to keep down. Since I was on my cereal diet, there weren't any dishes in the sink. I tended to use the same bowl over and over—rinsing it after I finished. The only visible sign of my blue funk were a few books and papers on the coffee table and a stack of DVD's on the floor I'd been marathon watching.

My phone began to ring. I turned the volume on the television down so I could hear if the caller was going to leave a message. The mechanical greeting came on, only to be greeted by the sound of the dial tone. *Another hang-up*, I thought. Those had been coming in quite frequently.

"You need to shake this, girl," I said out loud. "You have to make yourself move on." I shook my head as if I were shaking off the feeling of dread I was experiencing.

Suddenly the phone began to ring again. This time the caller left a message.

"Deeva, it's your Aunt Gabby. Baby, I thought some-one should tell you what's going on here. Your daddy is in the hospital—" Before she could get another word out, I grabbed the phone and hit the TALK button.

"What's wrong with my daddy, Auntie?"

"Hey, baby. He had to be rushed to the hospital the other night. I kind of figured your mama didn't call you."

I let my head fall back on the sofa and closed my eyes. "What hospital is he in?"

Aunt Gabby gave me all the information I needed to get in contact with him.

"Deeva, I really think you should come home so you can talk with his doctors and see what's going on with him. Your mama didn't want anybody to know he was in there, so you know she's not telling the family anything about his condition."

The most I could do was breathe a heavy sigh. My mother could be a real piece of work.

"I'll call the hospital and see what they'll tell me, and I'll call you back."

We said our good-byes and I hung up. I immediately began to dial the number she had given me. Once I was put through to his room, I waited for him to answer but was disappointed when Mommy Dearest picked up.

"Why didn't you call me?"

"Hello?"

"It's Deeva."

"What do you mean, why didn't I call you? Last time I checked, Charles was my husband. Not yours."

"He's also my father and I have the right to know if something is wrong with him."

I could hear her shifting something around.

"Mom?"

"What do you want, Deeva?"

"I can see I'm not getting anywhere with you. I don't know what it is I've done to you, but for once in my lifetime, can you think about how I feel?"

There was a long pause before I heard her say something. She evidently had placed her hand over the mouthpiece of the phone so I couldn't hear what she was saying.

"Look, I need to talk to the doctors. I have to go." Without another word, she hung up the phone on me.

I closed my eyes and took a deep breath as I thought of what I had to do next. As bad as I was feeling, I had no other choice but to do what Aunt Gabby said. I placed the phone on the table and went in search of my laptop.

I logged onto Delta's website. "Let's see what they have leaving out today."

CHAPTER 32

"How's everything with your dad?"

"He's in better spirits today. The doctors said he should be able to go home in a day or two." They're saying his heart attack was stress induced. I would've bet everything I had that my mother was behind it.

"That's good."

I sipped the remaining contents from the coffee cup. "Quincy, you know I really appreciate you calling and checking on me, but you don't have to."

"Oh, it's nothing. What's that song by Dionne Warwick and her friends?"

I could hear the beginning rifts of Stevie's harmonica as I thought about the song he was talking about. I couldn't do anything but smile.

"Yeah, but it seems like your being friends with me has cost you a couple of your old friends."

"The only one I have a problem with is Lorenzo's bitch ass. If it weren't for Tristan, I don't think any of us would deal with his henpecked ass. That's not a loss when you really look at it."

"Hasn't he been part of the crew from the beginning?"

"Hell naw. Tristan met him in college."

I shook my head and grabbed my shades from my purse. "Well, my friend. I'm on my way over to the hospital. I try to get there before my mother so we can have a nice quiet visit."

"Has your mother always been such a…" He paused as if he was either looking for the right words to describe what he was thinking, or waiting on my permission to call my mother what many had dubbed her.

"No, she hasn't always been a bitch." I laughed.

"Then what happened? Did you make a bad grade in a class or something?"

I laughed at his attempted humor. "Not exactly. I don't know. She sort of changed after my brother died."

"Ah, man. That's sad. Was he older or younger?"

"He was younger than me."

"How long ago did this happen?"

I punched the down button on the elevator. I was caught off guard by my reflection in the shiny elevator doors. A hint of sadness crossed my face as I thought about Cameron, my little shadow.

"He died when I was fourteen. So that's what? Sixteen years ago. He would've been twenty next month."

I stepped on the empty elevator.

"What did he die from?"

"Leukemia."

We were both quiet for a moment.

"So, if he died from a disease, why does your mom act like she blames you or something?"

"Like I said before, it's a long story and I don't have the time to really get into it now."

"I hear ya. Well, tell your pops I said to get better so he can come back to visit. This time, we're going to Strokers."

"Negro, please. My daddy ain't going to no strip club." I laughed at the very thought of Daddy stuffing dollar bills into to some chick's g-string.

"Don't cock block."

I laughed into the phone. "Whatever. I'll talk to you later."

"You do that. Oh, Deeva?"

"Yes?"

"It sounds really good to hear you laugh again."

I smiled. It had been a minute since I'd had a reason to laugh, or smile.

"Bye, Quincy." I hung up the phone.

The concierge greeted me as I made my way through the lobby and out the door. My rental car was waiting at the curb for me. I gave the valet a tip and jumped in.

"How are you today, Daddy?" I kissed him on the forehead.

"Oh, I'm feeling okay."

"Well, you look good." I moved a couple of books he

had in the chair to another one near the bed so I could sit down.

"Have you been over to the house?"

I looked at him sideways. "Why would I go over there? You're in here."

"Deeva, I need you and your mother to stop this. You would think she was your stepmother instead of the woman who carried you for nine months."

"Daddy, now you know it's a lost cause."

He shook his head and took a deep breath.

"Speaking of Cruella."

"Deeva, behave."

I laughed. I knew how to get under Daddy's skin.

"You're not funny."

"You know you love me." I picked up the remote and began to click through the channels, only to find much of nothing. We settled on a rerun of *Sanford and Son*. The end of the second episode was on by the time Mother appeared, ending the blissfulness we were enjoying.

"Honey," she sang as she opened the door.

I sat up in the chair.

"Oh. When did you get here?" she asked dryly.

"Hello, Mother. I'm glad to see you, too."

"I hope you're not in here stressing your father. He needs to get his rest." She placed her bag in the other chair on the opposite side of the room.

I gave Daddy one of those "see what I'm talking about" looks.

"You still didn't answer my question, Deeva."

I rolled my eyes. "What question was that?"

"When did you get here?"

"I've been here for two days."

"Two days?"

I nodded and kept watching the television.

"When are you leaving?"

"When Daddy goes home, I guess."

She was quiet for another moment before the doctor walked in.

"Mr. McCoy, how are we today?"

"Well, Doc, I'm not sure about you, but I happen to feel fine."

The doctor laughed and pulled my father's chart from the wall where the nurses kept it.

"You're right. It says so right here." He pointed to the chart. "Looking at the results of the EKG, I think we can get you out of here soon." He closed the chart and walked over to the bed, where he began to check his vital signs.

I grabbed my purse. "I'm going to go down to the vending machine for something to drink. I'll be back."

"You can go down to the nurses' station and they'll give you something to drink," the doctor said as he winked at me.

My mother stepped into his line of view. "How come you've never told me that before, Dr. Sailas?"

"Well, Mrs. McCoy, you've never mentioned you were thirsty any of the other times I was here." He went back to checking my father.

I looked at my mother, smiled and shook my head

before walking out. It was just like her; to think every man wanted her.

As I stood at the elevator rummaging through my purse for my wallet, she walked up behind me.

"You know he's been making passes at me since your father got here."

I looked back at her like she was crazy and turned my attention back to the front. "If you say so."

"Oh, I know so."

I shook my head again.

"What's so funny? Did someone tell a joke?"

"You're the joke, Mom. Your husband is in the hospital and all you can think about is the doctor flirting with you. A man who is not only young enough to be your son, but who seems to have no interest in you whatsoever."

She chuckled. "So what? You think he was flirting with you?"

"I'm not thinking anything about him, beyond him tending to Daddy." I stepped on the elevator and she followed.

"You waltz in here like you're Ms. High and Mighty or something. Like I can't take care of *my* husband."

"Your husband?"

"Yes, my husband."

"The same husband you've cheated on, let's see…" I pretended to be counting off in my head. "More times than both of our fingers and toes combined."

She had the nerve to seem shocked.

"Yes, Mother. I know about your little indiscretions. You know, when you used to pretend we were going to a friend's house. It was a friend, alright."

"You're talking nonsense."

"Oh, I know of what I speak. Let's see, what was his name?" I cocked my head to the side and searched my memory for a second. "Earl. Yeah, the one who had the daughters named Amy and Sharon."

Her mouth was slightly ajar.

"I remember this one time we were there and it got really late and Amy, Sharon and I had fallen asleep in the family room. I kept hearing something so I got up to investigate. Can you imagine the horror I felt when I found my mother and this man butt ass naked doing something I had never seen before?"

She turned her head in shame.

"Yeah, you were so busy doing your thing you never saw me. I eased out of there and went back to where the other girls were and forced myself to fall back to sleep. When I woke up the next morning in my own bed, I thought it had been a dream. A dream." I laughed. "But, I knew what I'd seen. Then it was confirmed when I overheard you talking to one of your girlfriends on the phone. Bragging about how good it was. You've always treated me like I was invisible to you; even when I was actually there."

"So, I had a couple of friends. I can't help it if your father isn't man enough to keep me at home."

If she hadn't been my mother, I would've slapped her silly, but I restrained myself from stooping to her level.

"Always working, or flying off here and there. I didn't get married to be left alone. When he was home, he was always fawning over you. Deeva this and Deeva that. I swear he acted as if he loved you more than me. So, yes, I've had other men in my life. Is that what you wanted to hear? I'm a philandering whore."

"You have never spoken any truer words in my life." I stepped away from her and walked into the cafeteria.

"I will not have you talking to me in such a way, Deeva. I am your mother."

I spun around and walked toward her real fast.

"My mother? You gave up that position in my life after Cameron died. Don't you remember? It should've been me; not him."

"What?" Her hand was over her chest, as if I'd hurt her heart.

"You asked God why He didn't take me, the other one. If He had to take any of your children, why couldn't it have been Deeva? Not your precious son. Your baby."

She stood there and didn't say a word.

"So, you see, you killed me sixteen years ago when you put Cameron in the ground. Far as I'm concerned, I never have to see you again. I wouldn't if it weren't for Daddy.

"How he manages to stay with a self-serving, self-centered alcoholic is beyond my imagination. I know one thing for sure, if I had my way, he would leave you and never look back."

I looked her up and down, my eyes full of disgust. I slowly turned and walked away, leaving her to think about all I had said.

CHAPTER 33

"Where is she?"

"She's in Florida. Her father had a mild heart attack and was in the hospital, so she went home to see about him." Quincy continued to study the table for a good shot.

"And you know this how?"

He crouched over the table and focused on his aim.

"Because I called to see if she was okay," he said, before striking the ball with the tip of his stick.

"What I can't understand is, why you calling his girl?" Lorenzo asked.

Quincy stood upright after his intended shot sank into the pocket he'd called.

"What's it to you?"

"I'm just saying."

"Just saying what? A bunch of nothing? If you know what's best for you, Lorenzo, you'd mind your own business."

"Mind my business? You're the one who's checking for my man's girl."

Quincy picked another ball and pocket and shot it in.

Tristan had begun to grow tired of the constant bickering between the two. One was pro-Deeva and the other wasn't. He hadn't quite figured which one he was himself, until the incident a few weeks ago. As much as he'd tried to get her out of his system and act as if he didn't care whether or not he ever saw her again, when he did, he knew he still loved her.

The only problem he had now was getting her to forgive him. He'd called her a few times, but when her answering machine picked up, he would hang up.

"Q, when's the last time you talked to her?"

"Earlier today." He shrugged his shoulder like it was nothing.

Tristan studied his body movement and noticed how he seemed to get uncomfortable with the line of questioning. His usual cocky stance was suddenly more reserved. With each question, he looked less at Tristan; trying to avoid any type of eye contact with him.

"Did she happen to mention when she was coming back?"

Quincy shrugged his shoulders again as he hunched over the table to knock in another ball.

Tristan continued to watch him. He couldn't quite put his finger on it, but he felt there was something going on that Quincy wasn't telling him.

"Yo, I'm out. I'll catch you cats later." Tristan dapped and hugged everyone.

"I'm out, too," Quincy said as he sank the eight ball

to win the game. He placed the pool stick back in the rack on the wall.

After saying their good-byes, Tristan and Quincy walked out to their cars.

"Tristan, I hope you're not upset about me being in contact with Deeva, but you know I've been rooting for her since I met her. I mean, you've had other women you've dealt with, but I've always felt Deeva was special."

Tristan looked at him. "I can't stop her from talking to you. I haven't been the man she needs lately, so I guess she had to talk to someone."

"Yeah, man." Quincy laughed. "I want ya'll to make it though."

I bet you do, Tristan thought to himself.

"Q."

"What's up?"

"If you find out when she's coming back, let me know."

"Oh, for sure." He gave him dap and walked to his car.

As he was leaving, Tristan noticed Quincy on his cell as he drove by him. He began to wonder if he was talking to Deeva. Was he losing her? To Quincy? How in the hell did that happen?

He pulled out his phone.

"Hello?"

"May I speak to Ebonee?"

"This is she."

He took a deep breath before telling her it was him. He wasn't sure what type of reaction he was going to get.

"It's Tristan."

"I know."

Seeing how she had answered and hadn't hung up yet, he felt it was safe to go on.

"How are you?"

"You don't have to make small talk with me. Just get to the point."

He had almost forgotten how straightforward she was.

"I heard about Deeva's father and I wanted to know if everything was okay."

"Then why didn't you call Deeva? I'm sure she would be a better source of information than me."

"You know why I didn't call her."

"I also know you didn't call me to find out about her father."

"You got me. I want to know what's going on with her and Q. He's been going on and on about her and honestly, it's bothering me."

Ebonee was silent for a moment. She'd already had a conversation with Deeva about how much time she had been spending with Quincy. Talking on the phone and what not. It was only a matter of time before one of them started catching feelings for the other and she didn't care what Tristan did to her, that wasn't cool.

"Well, I've been told he has been a really good source of comfort with all you two have been through. You know…someone she can talk to."

"That's what ya'll are for. You and Cara."

Ebonee laughed at his jealousy.

"See, sometimes a woman feels she needs a man's point of view to help her figure things out. Quincy has been her male perspective. Besides, he's always assuring her things are going to be okay, if she gives it time." Ebonee thought she'd ease his thoughts.

"That's the story he's giving me."

"Don't you believe him?"

Tristan paused for a moment and thought about it.

"I guess you don't, but I can't blame you. You seem to hang around with men who're really little girls."

"What do you mean by that?"

Ebonee blew out a frustrated breath.

"Come on, Tristan. Your friend and his girlfriend couldn't wait to throw shit in the game for Deeva. She wanted you to be with her friend so bad; they came back and gave you only a half truth of information. Let's not forget how you decided to handle the information once you got it. You could've handled the situation better than you did, instead of trying to showboat in front of people. Deeva deserved better than that."

"You're right about the last part. I should've had that conversation when we were alone, but I let my hurt and anger guide me."

"Why am I only right about that part? Your friend—"

"I didn't get that information from Lorenzo or Fallon."

"Then who told you?"

Tristan remembered the fallout between them and

Lisa and wondered if he should just leave well enough alone.

"You might as well tell it, because I think I have an idea who it is now."

"Lisa called me. I thought she wanted me to help her make things right between her and Deeva. Instead, she gave me an earful of information she thought I was entitled to."

"That sneaky bitch. Lord, please forgive me. I'm working on being a better person, but that was the lowest of low."

"Now you answer me something."

"What?" Ebonee asked.

"You said I only knew half of the truth. What's the actual truth then?"

"Yes, Deeva has a business where she investigates men for their significant others. It's something she's been good at for as long as I've known her and she makes a very good living doing it. Now, you have to realize she has to keep anonymity to protect herself, so it's not something she talks about with anyone."

"We were about to get married."

"I understand and she had plans to tell you. I guess the time was never right. Now, the part about your old girlfriend."

"She was never my girlfriend."

"Okay, okay. I believe you, but when she came in to see Deeva, that was the story she gave. Mind you, this was after you and Deeva had spent the weekend together. Deeva didn't know what to do. I guess you can say, you had rocked her world for three days straight."

Ebonee listened closely, trying to gauge his reactions to her words.

"I think Deeva said something about questioning you and you gave all the right answers, so she dropped it."

Tristan thought back to the night when they'd first started seeing each other, when Deeva had asked those weird questions. Now he knew why.

"So, our meeting wasn't some kind of setup for an investigation?"

"Did you not just hear me?"

"But Lisa said—"

"Don't tell me about what *Lisa* said. Have you forgotten the drama that's going on between Deeva and Lisa? Isn't it obvious Lisa is jealous of Deeva and would do anything to ruin her happiness?"

Tristan started to think of how he had been played. Lisa had done what she had set out to do. She had lured him into the middle of something that had been brewing for months, if not years. If she hadn't called, he and Deeva would've been married by now and living in marital bliss.

"Damn, I feel like a fool." He slammed his fist on the steering wheel.

"You should. Your behavior as of late has been less than stellar and downright selfish."

"Ebonee, I need you to be honest with me. Do I still have a chance?"

"Do you still love her?"

"Yes," he answered without any hesitation.

"Then there's a chance. I'm not saying it's going to be easy, but your love should make you willing to do whatever it takes to get her back."

"Whatever it takes, I'll do it."

"Then, I think we need to get to work."

"We?"

"Yes, because for all the wrongs you've committed lately, I know you really love Deeva. I knew it was only a matter of time before you came back from your trip to madness."

They both laughed.

"Do you think she still loves me?"

Ebonee paused, more for effect than anything else. He deserved to sweat a little. To think he had almost messed up to the point where it was possible he would lose her.

"Tristan, I know with all honesty that she does. How long she'll feel this way? Well, that's up to you."

"Let's get started then. I plan on us being in love forever."

CHAPTER 34

I closed my eyes as the plane began to cut through the clouds for the last leg of the flight. I had passed the hour and ten minutes by reading a book. Now I sat thinking about how it was time for me to get back to business once I got back to Atlanta. I'd played hooky from my life long enough and any successful business owner knows you have to mind your business yourself if you want to remain successful. Not saying Cara and Lonnie hadn't been holding things down in my absence.

Before leaving Florida, I wanted to make sure Daddy was going to be okay, so I stayed long enough to go to his first doctor's visit. After getting a clean bill of health from his doctor, I was satisfied. During that time, I didn't see Mother once, which was fine with me. The less interaction I had with her, the better.

The flight attendant interrupted my thoughts as she began the routine landing instructions. I let my seat back up to an upright position and put the tray table away.

For the first time since I'd gotten on the flight to Florida, I thought about Tristan. Wondered what he was doing. Was he thinking about me? Did he try to contact me at home while I was gone?

Girl, you're going to drive yourself crazy.

I realized this was another part of my life I was going to have to deal with once I got back. Good or bad, it was time to move on. Move on. Was I ready to move on? I hadn't given it much thought.

The plane dropped a little, causing my stomach to do a slight flip. I gripped the armrest out of reaction. Then suddenly my mind was flooded with a crazy thought. If this plane were to crash right now, had I enjoyed my life? Had I lived it close enough to the fullest where I wouldn't have any regrets? Did I fight for everything I wanted?

Once again, my mind went to Tristan. I had been truly happy when I was him. I thought about T.J. and the promise I'd made to him. A promise I hadn't honored lately in my attempt to ease my own pain. Trying to avoid Tristan had become more of a task than I wanted to deal with. I stopped getting T.J. as much as I once did, to take him on our little outings.

My eyes began to water as I thought about the disappointment T.J. must have felt every time I canceled on him. We still talked on the phone every day. I wanted to make sure he was doing okay.

Did you fight for everything you wanted? rang loudly in my head. Had I really given my situation with Tristan a fair chance? Once I thought about it, I knew the answer was no. No because I started things out deceiving him. Had I been honest from the beginning about all the important things, our relationship may have had a fighting chance.

The plane dropped again. I looked out the window and was both amazed and afraid at the rate of speed we were cutting through the clouds. I kept my eyes glued to the window, wondering when I would see the ground. Five minutes later, we broke through the turbulence and the pilot began to slow down.

Another safe landing, I thought as my body began to relax.

Twenty minutes later, I was boarding the train headed for baggage claim and my car. The whole way through the airport, I thought about one thing—was I going to go after Tristan or let the entire thing go. Maybe my train of thought would improve once I got some food in my system. Then I would take it to the council—Ebonee and Cara—and see what we could come up with.

CHAPTER 35

Tristan and Ebonee had begun to hash out their plan to get him back into Deeva's good graces. He knew it was going to have to be drastic and Ebonee was making sure that's exactly what it was.

"Did you get the flowers?" she asked as she poked around in the bags he'd placed on the kitchen counter.

"I did one better." He held up another bag and handed it to her.

"Oh-kay now. Rose petals in a bag. I'm impressed, Mr. Savage." She handed them back to him.

"What time did she say her plane was arriving?"

Ebonee looked down at her watch. "About ten minutes ago." Suddenly her cell began to ring. The caller ID registered Deeva's name and number.

"Damn!"

"What?"

"She's calling me. I hope her plane didn't land earlier than we expected."

"We're almost done, so stall her if you have to." Tristan felt a sudden spike of panic. What if she was coming down the street? Would she be angry when she found him there?

Ebonee walked into another room to talk while Tristan continued to set out the last of the preparations. He wanted to make sure everything was just right. More than just right—perfect.

Ebonee returned from the bedroom five minutes later.

"What'd she say?"

"She wants me to meet her here so we can talk about you."

Tristan stopped what he was doing and looked at Ebonee, who had a smile plastered on her face. He took that as a good sign.

"How much longer do we have before she gets here?" He checked the pots on the stove one last time before turning them down on low.

"She's coming through the terminal now so I'd say a good thirty to forty minutes." Ebonee looked down and checked her watch. "What else do we have to do?"

"Everything is pretty much done. The only thing left is the patio."

"Then let's go." She rolled the carryon bag she brought over to the back door.

Together they transformed her back patio into a perfect romantic setting. Lit candles outlined the path from the backdoor to the gazebo where a dinner setting of fine china for two was prepared. A fresh floral arrangement was the centerpiece.

Ebonee zipped her bag up and straightened up her back.

She looked over at Tristan who was lighting the last candle on the table. "Well, the rest is up to you from this point."

He took a cleansing breath, pulling air deep into his lungs.

"You think this will work?"

"I think she'll at least stop and listen to what you have to say. So, that gives you an in. Now, what happens from there is all on you."

He followed her back into the house.

"Can you call her and see how close she is while I run upstairs to finish getting ready?"

Ebonee grabbed her phone.

Tristan stood in the upstairs bathroom mirror, giving himself a pep talk as he finished putting on his after-shave—Unforgivable—a favorite scent of Deeva's.

"You can do this, man. Tell her how much you love her and how you want to make a life with her. How empty yours has been without her."

"Tristan," Ebonee called up the stairs.

"I'm coming now."

"She's pulling up in the driveway, so hurry up."

He ran his hand over his head one last time and rushed down the stairs. Ebonee winked at him as he walked out the back door to wait by the gazebo for Deeva. His heart was pounding so loudly he thought the neighbors could hear it. The only thought running through his mind was whether or not she would walk through the backdoor. The only thing he could do now was hope, pray, and wait.

CHAPTER 36

I felt as if I had been traveling for hours by the time I reached my house. The many thoughts I had running through my mind on the plane were still plaguing me as I sat in my driveway. I was more than happy when Ebonee agreed to meet me at the house to talk. I really wanted to get things worked out before it started to drive me crazy.

"Crazy, huh." I smiled as I pulled my bags out of the car and slowly rolled them to the front door. Since I knew Ebonee was inside, I decided to ring the doorbell instead of fishing around in my purse for my front door keys. I wasn't like most people who kept all their keys on the same keychain. Ebonee seemed to take her time about getting there. I leaned on the button again.

"I'm coming. I'm coming." She clicked off the dead-bolt and then the bottom lock.

"What took you so long?"

"Took me so long? I was expecting you to use your key. This is *your* house."

"As long as it took you to open the door, I should've

used my keys, but my hands are kinda full." I pointed to the three bags I had in my possession.

She grabbed the larger bag and pulled it inside. I placed the other bags down once I got inside and followed her into the kitchen. While stretching my back, I noticed she had her purse on her shoulder.

"Where you going?"

"Look, I know you want to talk, but I feel I'm not the person you need to talk to." She motioned toward the back door. "Now, before you start to trip, we were here before you called and asked me to meet you over here. This was his idea and since you wanted to talk about him, I'm thinking the two of you were somehow mentally on the same page." She gave me a kiss on the cheek.

"Welcome back, friend. Now, go out there and get your man." She pushed me toward the door and walked in the opposite direction to leave.

I stood there for a moment. Fear was slowly becoming my friend. Thinking about him and talking about him was easier than this. It would've given me the time I needed to get my thoughts together. Have whatever it was I wanted to tell him together. Now, I was being forced to wing it.

Or just go with the flow and say what's in your heart.

I took a deep breath and placed my hand on the door. *You can do this.* Slowly, I followed the trail of candles out to the gazebo where I found him. His all-white ensemble softened my reserve and chipped away at the attitude I had brought outside with me.

This is your chance to see if it's worth the fight.

"This is really nice." I stood across the table from him. I could see the worry in his face lessen.

"I remembered us talking about having a romantic dinner out here once and thought, what better occasion than this." He walked around the table to where I was standing and pulled out my chair. I gave him a tight-lipped smile and sat down. He walked over to his side again and joined me. We sat staring at each other for a while. Neither one of us wanting to break the spell we seemed to have fallen into.

Tristan cleared his throat.

"Would you like a glass of wine?" He held up a bottle of my favorite—Lambrusco.

I nodded my head yes, watched as he poured some into my glass and then some into his.

I looked around the patio and noticed the food warmers on the other side near the grill.

"Would that be dinner?"

"Yes it is. Prepared by yours truly."

I beamed a real smile this time.

"You don't know how grateful I am right now. I am starving. You know those no-frills airlines don't give you anything to eat *or* drink."

"Then let me do something about that." He got up and returned with two plates of lasagna and placed them on the table. Before he sat down, he went back over to where the food was and returned with two smaller plates of salad.

"I hope you were in the mood for pasta."

I smiled again. This time a little laugh escaped.

"I'm always in the mood for pasta."

He gave me a seductive wink.

"I know."

We continued with our pleasantries as we enjoyed the rest of our meal. Once the food on my plate was gone, I felt we had danced around the subject of us long enough and it was time to get down to the business at hand.

"Why didn't you talk to me first before deciding to embarrass the hell out of me on the eve of one of the most important days of my life?"

My line of questioning caught him totally by surprise as he tried to finish chewing and swallowing the last bit of his food. He shrugged his shoulders first.

"I was angry and hurt. It felt as if I had been played."

"Played? You thought I played you? Did it ever occur to you that I was about to marry you? If you were being played, we would've never made it to that point."

"I wanted to hurt you like I was hurting."

"Well, your mission was accomplished." I took another sip of my wine. "I can't believe you would believe your friend when you knew him and his girlfriend never wanted us to be together in the first place."

"They weren't the ones who told me."

I gave him a look of bewilderment. "Who told you then? Octavia?"

He shook his head.

I thought about it for a while and couldn't think of anyone else. "Then who?"

He hesitated for a moment.

"Who, Tristan?"

He took a deep breath before giving me his answer. "Lisa."

It took my brain a minute to wrap around what he'd said.

"Lisa?" I was stunned, but then again she had become capable of anything lately.

"I called Octavia to see if it was true."

I ran through a mental ticker tape of thoughts about Lisa. I wondered if I had done or said anything to cause her to go out of her way to hurt me. I couldn't remember a day in my life without Lisa in it, up until recently.

"Deeva?"

My head snapped up and I looked at him. He rose from his seat and came around to me.

"I'm sorry. We can rehash this over and over all night and the outcome will still be the same, but that's not what I want. What I want is for us to start over fresh. Actually…" He got down on his knee in front of me. "I want us to start over where we should be. Where we would be at this moment, if I hadn't allowed other people to meddle in our affairs. I know I played a part in it, too, but, baby, I'm willing to admit I was wrong, because the bottom line is, I can't live without you another second.

"I think about you every day. I don't want to have to

wonder what you're doing and who you're with. I want to know what you're doing and know, because you're with me." He reached into his pocket.

"I know you gave it back to me, but this ring was meant for you." He opened the box and my mind began to race.

Was I ready for this again? Would we make it to the altar this time?

"You don't have to rush your decision, but if I have things my way, we can get married tomorrow. I don't care, as long as you marry me." He slid the ring on.

I looked down at my finger. The ring felt as if it was supposed to be there.

"We can go in the morning," I said, trying to call his bluff.

"Okay. I think the courthouse opens around eight or so. We can leave here and get down there around seven and have a little breakfast before we go."

"You're serious, huh?"

"Baby, I almost lost you once. I don't plan on losing you again."

I looked into his eyes for a hint of something. Something saying he was going to run again. Something saying he was unsure. There wasn't a hint of either. What I found instead was a man who was serious. A man who loved me and no matter how much I may have wanted to fight it, I loved him, too.

"Now, if you want, we can have a wedding with everything planned out like before, but it's going to take that much longer—"

"We can go tomorrow. I'll call Ebonee and have her meet us down there to be a witness. Then, maybe in a year or two, we'll have a big ceremony."

He jumped up and pulled me into a tight embrace before kissing me so hard and deep, it was as if I was supplying him with the very oxygen he needed to breathe.

"I haven't had sex—" He stopped in mid-sentence and looked at me.

"Look, I just agreed to marry you. If we're going to move forward, we have to put all of that in the past. It hurt, but you already know that."

"I didn't sleep with her, Deeva."

"I never said you did."

He wrapped his arms around me tighter. I returned the gesture.

"Now, what were you about to say before? Because I know I haven't had sex in…" I closed one eye and looked up as if I was counting.

"Two months, three weeks, and five days," Tristan answered for me.

I looked at him.

"Don't be surprised. If I'm not mistaken, the last time you had sex was with me."

"Are you sure about that?" I thought I'd play with him a bit.

"What do you mean, am I sure? I hope I'm sure."

"You hope?"

"Why you playing with me? I'm sure. I'm damn sure of it." He kissed my neck.

"Now that you're *sure* about it, what are you going to do about it?"

"Oh, I know exactly what to do about it." He grabbed me by my hand and led me back into the house.

No sooner than the door closed behind us, he was undressing me—pulling my shirt over my head. I kicked off my shoes to help speed up the process. I could feel his hardness against my stomach.

"Damn, baby, I miss you," he whispered against my ear.

"I missed you, too," I responded in between kisses. I hadn't realized how much I missed him until this moment. His touch was driving me wild.

He was kissing me and walking backward toward the couch.

"No. Not here. I want to go upstairs to the bedroom," I said in a half-whisper.

Without another word, he ushered me up the stairs and into the bedroom. By this time *his* clothes were off—a trail leading up the stairs. His hands were all over me and it felt good.

"Baby, I feel like I'm about to explode."

And he did. Numerous times that night.

As I lay nestled up in his arms later that night, I thought back on the thoughts I'd had earlier on the plane. Before today, I hadn't fought for us. I had been content to let things just happen, but not anymore. From this moment forward, I was going to make sure I gave it my all before I ever walked away again.

Tristan kissed me on the back of my neck.

"What are you thinking about?"

"How tomorrow, around this time, I'll be Mrs. Tristan Savage."

"That you will, baby. That you will."

CHAPTER 37

"Here's to the happy couple." Cara raised her glass and everyone joined in.

"Man, I'm glad you got it together. You had me scared there for a little while."

Tristan looked at Quincy. "You had me scared, too."

"Why?"

"I guess my insecurities were getting the best of me, but I'm glad to see I had you all wrong."

Quincy gave Cara a tight squeeze and then kissed her. They had been secretly seeing each other, after meeting at the first get-together we had at Ebonee's. After things kind of blew up between Tristan and me, they decided to keep their relationship on the low until we were able to work things out.

I pulled Ebonee to the side.

"See, you were thinking the same thing as Tristan, but it wasn't me he was interested in."

"Well, I wasn't the only one who felt that way, so I don't feel so bad."

Lonnie walked over and handed me a plate.

"Lonnie, I can't thank you enough for putting this together."

He hugged me and then air kissed me on both cheeks. "Anything for you, boss lady. Besides, this is what I do. Speaking of, I want to sit down and talk with you about starting my own business." He waited for my response.

"Do you have a business plan?"

"Yes." He waited with baited breath for my answer.

"When I get back from my honeymoon, we'll sit down and talk and see about getting the ball rolling for you."

In true Lonnie fashion, he pulled out his theatrics. A hand pressed against his chest, he acted as if he would burst from the joy he was feeling.

"Okay, gurl."

"Go somewhere and sit down." I hip checked him as I walked away to find my husband and son.

"Deeva, can you come here for a second."

I walked over to the table where Tristan's parents were sitting.

"Yes, Ma'am?"

Mrs. Savage grabbed my hand.

"I didn't get a chance to talk to you yet. Come. Sit." She patted the chair next to her and I obeyed. "I'm so glad you kids finally got things together. You had me worried there for a minute."

"Yeah, me too," Mr. Savage piped in.

I had to fight back my urge to burst into laughter as I watched him devouring his meal.

"Well, I wanted to welcome you into the family."

"Don't you mean we?" he asked.

"She knows that, Honey." She waved her hand to quiet him.

"Anyway, I want you to know you didn't just marry our son—you married a family. From this moment forward, we are Mom and Dad to you."

I could feel my emotions coming to the forefront. Unlike me, Tristan had a real family. A mother and father who honestly loved each other, and their children. Not some phony front put on at certain times for the sake of appearances.

I got up to give them each a hug.

"Thank you. This really means the world to me." I paused and looked at them. The love in their eyes shone through.

"Can I have my wife back now? Don't believe anything they say, baby." Tristan kissed me and pulled me closer to him.

"You go on somewhere with that mess. We just wanted to talk to our new daughter."

"Baby, it's almost time for us to get out of here."

"Where's T.J.?"

"I'm right here." He walked up beside me and put his arm around my waist.

"I know ya'll ain't taking that boy on your honeymoon with ya?"

"No, Daddy. He's going to stay with you and Mama until we get back."

"Well, when are ya'll leaving? I couldn't wait to get

on my honeymoon. You remember that, don't ya, baby?" Daddy Savage winked at his wife and she blushed.

Tristan started pulling me away. "Okay, it's really time to go now."

"Hey, boy, don't you know that's how you got here?"

I hugged both of them before we walked off.

"Are you ready to go?"

"I'm ready when you are. Let me go tell my girls we're gone."

Before I walked away, he reeled me back into him. "Do you know how much I love you?"

"I have an idea, but you've got a long time to show me."

"Oh, and I'm going to show you, over and over." He kissed me with each "over" that he said.

"I'm going to hold you to that."

I walked away to find Ebonee and Cara.

Cara and Quincy were hugged up on the dance floor.

I was still shocked by that one. I was starting to think Quincy had an ulterior motive for hanging around and calling. He did, but not the one I thought.

"I'm not asking ya'll to stop what you're doing, but I wanted to let you know we're leaving."

They let go of each other to give me a hug.

"Where's my boy?"

I pointed to the other side of the room where Tristan was talking with Delante, Malik, and the others.

"We're going to go over and say good-bye while you make your rounds."

"I know you're not going that far, but I'm going to miss you." Cara gave me another tight squeeze.

"If you need me—which I know you won't—you have the numbers."

"Don't you worry about the office. Just go and enjoy yourself."

"Oh, I am."

I walked away from them, in search of Ebonee.

"Here you are." I sat down beside her.

"Well, you did it."

"Yes I did." I admired the rings on my finger. "I owe you a major thank you."

"Yes, you do."

There were two champagne glasses on her table from the toast earlier. I grabbed one and passed the other one to her.

"To friendship. Sometimes the best kind of sisters are the ones we get to pick."

"Here, here," she said as she touched glasses with me. "Now, get out of here. You should've been gone an hour ago."

"I know, but we were having so much fun."

"Yes, Lonnie outdid himself again."

We finished off the champagne.

"Are you drinking again? I'm going to really be able to take advantage of you tonight." Tristan leaned in and gave Ebonee a kiss on the cheek.

"Yeah, get your ol' liquor-head wife out of here."

"Damn, you would turn on me like that?"

She winked at me. "You know I got your back."

"Tristan, where's your friend and his girlfriend?"

I nudged her shoulder.

"What?"

"I thought it was best not to invite them, since my wife doesn't feel liked by them."

"Oh, don't blame it on me. I've got the rings and the signed paper. I could give a rat's ass about them liking me."

"Now you tell me."

"Would you two get out of here? You're going to lose your reservation."

"I don't think there's an influx of people checking into the Four Seasons Hotel on a Tuesday night."

"You tell 'em, baby."

Tristan gave me a high-five.

"Nice to see ya'll working together as a team."

"We'll see you on Sunday."

Tristan pulled me up from the table. We both gave her a hug and went to the front of the room.

Lonnie held up a finger, signaling us to wait as he walked over to the DJ booth where he was handed a mic.

"I know we've all been having a blast, but all good things must come to an end. It's time to bid the bride and groom farewell as they head off to their honeymoon. Let's give them another congratulatory clap as they head out the door." Everyone in the room began to clap and hug us as we walked out.

Lonnie walked us to the front door where a super-stretch limo was idling.

"You didn't!"

"Oh, girlfriend, you know it's nothing but the best for you." He kissed me good-bye and shook Tristan's hand.

"Now, go off and get started on expanding your family. I'm expecting you to be pregnant by Monday morning."

"You know you're crazy."

The driver held the back door open for us. I waved good-bye to Lonnie and slid into the car behind Tristan.

The driver got in, after securing us.

"There's a full bar, if you want something to drink."

"I think we've had more than enough to drink for one night." I was feeling a little lightheaded from the bubbly I had earlier.

"Umm, that means I should have no problem taking full advantage of you later."

"Oh, you didn't need liquor for that." I slid over closer to him.

"The ride isn't long enough," he said as he caressed my face.

"You know, once we get to the room and consummate our marriage, there's no turning back. You're stuck with me forever."

"I can live with that. Besides, I don't go fishing to throw them back." He gave me a kiss.

"Umm, I can't wait to get you in this room." I played with the buttons on his shirt.

"You mean suite."

"The only thing I'm worried about in that room is the bed."

"I guess I'm in for a long night then."

I thought about the goodie bag I'd packed earlier.

"Oh, you have no idea."

CHAPTER 38

Six Months Later

Things in my life couldn't have been better. Tristan and I had found a new house in the same neighborhood he was living in. This worked out great since we didn't want to take T.J. out of his routine or away from his friends. The house was a larger model though. The extra rooms were a blessing, seeing how we were going to need another bedroom in about four months. I guess Lonnie's premonition was right.

Tristan had gotten a promotion on his job that only lasted for about a month. He said he wasn't comfortable being a suit in the management department. Somehow, he worked out a deal where he could keep his pay raise and go back to driving.

I'd made plans to meet with Ebonee and Cara for lunch, but decided to surprise them with a boxed lunch from Proof of the Pudding in the office. Cara and I had been working really hard to expand DeCoys into the television arena.

I thought about the days I spent watching *The Mandrel Polk Show*. I felt as if I had come full circle in my professional life. The success of DeCoys allowed me to help Lonnie start his own business—which was doing very well. I have to admit we missed having him around the office every day, but he makes it his business to come to see us at least once a week.

The chime for the door out front went off. Thinking it was Ebonee, I walked out to greet her.

"It's about time you got here. I ordered you the Caribbean chicken wrap from the low-carb menu. You've been really good about staying on your diet." I was looking down at the menu I'd printed out from the computer as I was walking, but looked up when she didn't respond. I stopped dead in my tracks.

"I know you weren't expecting to see me." Lisa stood two steps away from me in the lobby.

I tried to will myself to say something, but couldn't find my voice.

"I'm not going to stay long, but I wanted to see you."

I gave her a partial smile.

Her eyes seemed a bit dull and her makeup was applied a little heavier than I'd ever seen her wear it.

"I see you're having a baby."

Instinctively, my hand went to my stomach.

"Who's the lucky man?"

I could hear the sarcasm in her voice, letting me know nothing had really changed.

I showed her the ring on my left hand. "My husband."

"Oh. You got married? I heard about what happened

with you and Tristan. I didn't expect you to run out and find someone new this fast." She gave off a nervous laugh.

"New? I guess you didn't see the name on the door, but here's a business card." I walked over to the receptionist's station and handed her one of my cards with my *new* last name. The look of astonishment on her face was priceless.

"So, he married you after all?"

"After all what? The effort you put into trying to ruin my life?"

She feigned a look of shock. "Me?"

"Cut the shit, Lisa. You'll lie to the end, won't you?"

"Lie about what?" She nervously adjusted her purse on her shoulder.

"Why are you here? Is it because Chauncey dumped you?"

Eyes stretched wide in shock, she shot me a "how did you know" look.

"I wouldn't say he dumped me."

"His wife is pregnant again and he's decided to make things work with her. Isn't that the story he gave you? Yeah, that's what she does. Every time she catches him messing around on her, she gets pregnant. It's her way of keeping him from leaving. If you want to know how many times he's been caught, count the number of kids they have behind the oldest one."

I realized I had hit it on the head, by the way she avoided looking me in the face.

"So, what did you accomplish, Lisa? You didn't win the man you thought was the prize. You didn't win at ruining my happiness. You might have delayed it a little, but you weren't successful at taking it completely."

"Deeva, we've been friends—"

I put my hand up to stop her.

"I know better than anyone how long we've been friends. Why do you think it bothers me so, that you would do these hurtful things to me? You were the friend I was supposed to grow old with."

"Are you sure that's how you saw me? Or was it Ebonee you saw in the chair right next to you?"

I shook my head.

"I kind of figured you were jealous of Ebonee, but you had no reason to be. We were all a part of the circle."

She looked down at her feet for a moment and then back up at me.

"So what do we do to fix this?"

"Lisa, I've had time to think and really evaluate a few things in my life since our so-called friendship ended. After some serious soul searching, I can honestly say you have never really been my friend. I was the one who nurtured our relationship. You, on the other hand, have always done little conniving things to me. Like the time you started a rumor about me sleeping with an entire football team when we were in junior high. I couldn't believe it when I found out it was you who started such a nasty rumor. Do you remember what your response was when I asked you about it?"

She looked away in shame.

"You were mad with me because I didn't come to your house when I promised you I would. I wasn't home because my brother got sick and had to be rushed to the hospital. Besides, we were only thirteen. Do you know what I went through behind that? Of course you do. You were there when people were talking behind my back. Pointing and laughing as they called me out of my name."

"Like you said, we were thirteen. It was something a thirteen-year-old girl would do."

"To her best friend? How about the time you invited two boys I really liked to a party you were having? It was like you hoped I would get caught up in a situation. And when we were in college…"

"You always thought you were so much better than people. Sitting up on your pedestal like you were Ms. High and Mighty," she snapped.

"What are you talking about?"

"I'm a daddy's girl. Well, whoopty fucking do. Some of us didn't have our daddies at home."

"Is that what this is about? Because my daddy was a part of my life and your deranged-ass daddy wasn't? Your mother made up for anything your daddy would've been. You had the best mom in the world, but you don't see me giving your ass grief because mine never gave a shit about me. What I wouldn't have given to have Ms. Veronica as my mom."

She was quiet.

"All these years you've gone out of your way to hurt me because of my dad. Now who's the selfish one?"

Suddenly the door opened.

"Girl, I was—"

Lisa looked at Ebonee and then back at me.

"Hey, Lisa."

"Hi." She grabbed her purse strap tighter.

"You know, Lisa, I have plans and right now, you're cutting into them."

"Can we talk later then?"

"I think we've said all we have to say to one another."

"Damn, Deeva. You're going to just cut me off like that? We've been friends for what?"

"Twenty-five long years, which didn't mean a damn thing to you when you decided to get with Chauncey?"

"Usually you forgive me." She sounded as if she'd been wounded.

"Well, I guess we're getting too old to play the forgive-me game. You know, I read somewhere sometimes your closest friend is your worst enemy. After dealing with you all these years, I honestly believe it."

Her lip began to quiver. "I came because I needed you."

Ebonee laughed. "This is none of my business, so I'm going to go and wait in your office."

"I was wondering when you were going to leave."

"Bitch, don't get me started on your ass. Lord, please forgive me." She raised her eyes upward. "But I can't hold this in." She got up in Lisa's face. "Deeva is doing good to even talk to your ass. If it was me, I would've knocked the shit out of you. Coming up in here, asking for forgiveness? Please. You figured out you've burned so many bridges that nobody wants to be bothered with you and your shit."

"I'm out of here."

"Bounce," Ebonee called out.

"Lisa, I loved you like a sister, but you could never see that. Maybe one day I'll be able to get over what you've done, but I don't see it happening anytime soon." I walked over and opened the door for her.

She turned her nose up at Ebonee and me and walked out without looking back.

"The nerve of her, even showing her face around here. You okay?"

"Girl, I'm like Mary. My life is fine."

Cara came out of her office.

"Were ya'll arguing?"

"Look at Johnny Come Lately."

We laughed and walked into the kitchen where our lunch had been set out nicely. We filled Cara in on Lisa's visit as we ate.

"Damn, I was on a call and missed it."

"You didn't miss much."

"Oh, I found something, Deeva." She got up and went down the hall to her office and returned with a file.

"I know you've probably forgotten about this, but I came across it in some of Lonnie's old files."

I scanned over the contents. "Ooh. Damn."

"Yeah, I thought the same thing when I saw it."

"Lonnie is too good sometimes. How did he get this?"

"Get what?" Ebonee reached for the file and read over it. "Are you serious?!"

"What should I do?" I asked.

"Are they still acting shitty with you?"

"They were a bit cold the last time we invited them over for the housewarming party." I thought about the little snide remarks Fallon said about me trapping Tristan; after we announced we were expecting.

"Tristan put her in her place," Ebonee reminded me.

"Oh, you have to use this. Bring that bitch down a peg or two."

"This is serious. People could be hurt behind this." I took a bite out of my sandwich.

"She deserves it."

"Cara," Ebonee said.

"What?"

"There's a lot at stake here. Maybe you should talk to Tristan about it before you do anything."

"Just like Ebonee to be the adult about things. I say, for once, you should stoop down to her level and let her know you're not to be fucked with. Sorry, Ebonee." Cara patted her on the arm.

"Girl, you're okay. I let my religion go when that skank was here earlier."

We all laughed.

"If I were you, I'd make copies and mail them to her, let her know they're from you. That way the next time you see them, she'll be sure to be nicer to you."

I thought about the ammunition I had in my possession. This would definitely keep them either away altogether or put them on notice; like Cara said. So, don't fuck with me.

I would sit on it for a little while longer, but how long would depend on them.

CHAPTER 39

A few weeks later I had a surprise party for Tristan. Lonnie was on hand to make sure everything went smoothly.

"Lonnie, I haven't had a chance to talk to you, but how did you get this information?"

We were in my home office getting the last of the things we were going to need before Quincy met us at the restaurant with Tristan in a few hours.

"Oh, girl, that was easy. I did a background check. Got social security numbers, old high school information, and everything came together."

"You are bad. I'm starting to regret letting you leave."

"Now you know if you need me, I'm only a phone call away. Have you decided what you're going to do with it?"

"I was thinking about destroying it, but knowing their track record, I better keep it in case."

He reached over and placed his hand on my stomach. The baby began to move like it always did when he touched it.

"See, this baby is going to be crazy about me."

I placed the folder in the file drawer of my desk.

"Safe keeping.

"You ready, Mama?"

"Umm-hmm."

The surprise was a hit. He didn't expect a thing and was happy to see such a crowd out to celebrate with him. I told him we were going to the restaurant to eat and had everyone there waiting when we got there.

Lorenzo and Fallon arrived two minutes too late and missed the whole surprise. I was starting to get the feeling they had tried to arrive late in order to ruin things.

"Did you hear her?" Cara asked as she saddled up next to me in the booth.

"Hear who?"

"That bitch over there." She pointed to where Fallon was standing, talking to a couple of other women.

"No, what did she say?"

"She's still talking about Tristan being trapped by you. How he had called off the wedding before, but you got pregnant and he married you out of obligation. He was going to marry her friend, if you hadn't ruined things."

I could feel my blood begin to boil. As much as I had tried to be nice, I knew I had to do to her what I'd done to Lisa—put an end to the bullshit for once and for all.

I took a deep breath before getting up. Slowly, I walked up to her and her group for the evening.

"Are you having a good time, Fallon? You ladies having a good time?"

"Oh, Deeva. Yes, this was really nice. Even though we missed the surprise."

"Well, the invitation said be here by seven."

"I guess I read it wrong." She turned her back to me and shook her head.

"You know, I think I've been pretty nice to you, considering all things, but now I feel the need to set the record straight."

"Set the record straight?"

"Yes. First of all, Tristan asked me to marry him again. Our baby was conceived on our honeymoon. So, you need to stop walking around here telling people I trapped him."

"Oh, Deeva, it's not a big deal."

"No, it is a big deal. I can't help it if you can't seem to get Lorenzo down the aisle and I was able to get mine in what?"

"A little more than a year," Cara added.

"Now how is that possible? You've only been engaged for what? Three almost four, years? I would start to wonder if there was something wrong with me, too."

"I would too, Deeva."

"Lorenzo and I are saving for our wedding. So unlike you, I don't have to go down to the courthouse to be married."

"Don't kid yourself. If I wanted to, I could throw the

biggest wedding ever, but my man loved me so much, he couldn't wait to marry me, so we went down to the courthouse."

I could tell that I was getting under her skin.

"Now, back to you. Damn, three years and you haven't been able to save enough money yet? Hell, in three years, you should have enough money to have a wedding, a baby, and buy a new house."

"Naw, Deeva. I think there's another reason why she hasn't been able to close the deal."

I politely asked the women who had been her captive audience earlier to excuse us for a moment before I continued.

"I was thinking the same thing, Cara. I have an idea, but do you?" I looked at Fallon.

"An idea about what? You don't know anything about my business."

"But you seem to think you're the authority on mine. I'm only going to tell you this once: Stay the fuck outta my business, because what I know will turn your world upside down."

Cara and I were about to walk off when she opened her mouth again, in an attempt to get back at me for sending her audience away.

"Once again, you're talking out the side of your neck."

I slowly turned around and got up in her face.

"Cara, how does that song by Katy Perry go?" I could see Lorenzo approaching in my peripheral view. I smirked at him and turned back to Fallon.

On cue, Cara and I started to sing, "*I kissed a girl and I liked it…*"

"What are you talking about?" Fallon asked as she looked over at Lorenzo who seemed to be frozen in his tracks.

"Unless they legalize same sex marriages in the state of Georgia, you'll be waiting forever to get married."

I gave them both the once-over and walked away; my arm hooked into Cara's.

"That's how you do it," she said, only loud enough for me to hear. "I don't think you'll be having problems with either one of them from this point forward."

We looked back to find Fallon in tears headed for the exit and Lorenzo—better known as Lauren up until sixteen years ago—was right behind her.

"You know he's going to call Tristan?"

"Hey, they provoked you. Besides, I don't think she, I mean he, is going to call at all."

"How do you figure that?"

"He's gone through too much trouble to keep his past a secret. Do you really think he wants his boys to know once upon a time he was a she?"

"Maybe you're right, but Tristan is still going to wonder what happened."

"Then you tell him. You made a promise to never keep secrets from him. So, no matter how much you think it's going to hurt him, you have to tell him."

"Well, you make me a promise."

"What?"

"Don't say anything to Quincy. You know he's never really liked Lorenzo to begin with."

"And now we know why."

"What are you two scheming on over here?" Tristan walked up to me and I gave him a big hug.

"Oh nothing."

"Nothing at all," Cara added.

Ebonee and Lonnie came over, both wearing a knowing smile on their faces.

"Baby, you outdid yourself tonight. I haven't seen some of these people in years."

"So you like your surprise?"

"I love it. Just like I love you." He wrapped me in his arms and kissed me.

"Okay, now. Not in public. Ya'll know it's against the law to show any type of PDA."

"What the hell is PDA, Lonnie?"

"Public display of affection. Damn, Cara, what school did you go to?"

"Alright, Lonnie, we love you, but we'll double-team you, talking about our beloved alma mater."

"Don't make these panthers attack you," Ebonee said as we playfully surrounded Lonnie.

"Ooh, I'm scared."

"You better be," said Cara.

"Alright, ya'll leave Lonnie alone. Come and dance with me."

"All three of us?"

"Yeah. I think I'm man enough to handle the three of you."

I popped him upside his head playfully.

"I don't think so."

"Besides, my man is here." Cara walked away to find Quincy.

"I guess I have to settle for you then, Lonnie?"

"Settle for me? You say that like I'm some leftover piece of lunchmeat."

"Come on, crazy boy, and dance with me." Ebonee pulled him away.

As we were dancing cheek to cheek on the dance floor, Tristan leaned into my ear.

"I saw Lorenzo and Fallon hightail it out of here. I would ask what happened, but I think it has something to do with what was in the folder in your office."

I suddenly stopped dancing and looked at him wide-eyed. "You know?"

"I've known for a while now."

"And you remained friends with him, I mean her?"

"It bothered me at first, but I decided to let it slide. I enjoyed his friendship, regardless of what he was. Plus, I never thought anyone would find out, with all the effort he put forth to cover it up. He pretty much completely erased his past."

"We found out."

"That just goes to show, you're damn good at what you do. I better stay in line or I'm in trouble."

"I'm glad you know this." I kissed him long and hard.

I looked around the room and found the people who meant the world to me. As I looked at the whole scene, I thought back to where I was a little over a year ago. I thanked God for putting the change in my life I needed to get going. Who knows where I would've been right now if Evan had never let me go. I'd probably still be there miserable as hell.

They say change is hard and it's scary, but sometimes change is needed in order for you to keep going. Well, from this point forward, I would always welcome change in my life.

Acknowledgments

It's been three years since the release of my last book, *In the Midst of It All* and my life has been through some real changes. It's been almost two years since I suffered the loss of my mother. I lost my grandmother a few months ago, and a few weeks ago, my father-in-law passed away suddenly. As we gathered to say good-bye, I noticed all the things they'd accumulated which had been left behind. So, it got me to thinking…

In our lives we will win and lose, live and learn, love and hurt, but what really matters is the enjoyment we experienced and the lives we touched during our time here, because in the end, all the material things will only be "stuff" once we're gone.

Writing the acknowledgments are always the toughest for me. I always want to make sure I thank everyone who means anything to me, but in the process I always leave someone out. So, I thought this time I'd make it short, but I wanted to thank a special group of kids I've become acquainted with.

My children:

To the two I gave birth to, Calina and Ramzey. You

both know how much I love and appreciate you. No matter how old you get, you'll always be my babies. To the others I have gathered along the way—Victoria, Ellori, Steven (go Tech), Patrell, Bryan, and Tremaine (Trey). I mentioned all of you first because in some way or another, you have touched my life in a special way and made it that much better. I love you like my own.

To the rest of the clan, Walter, Christy, Shannon, Monique, Trevell, Tomori, Brionca, Korey, Ashley, Carla, Catrice, Jarred, Taylor, Simone, Joe W., and a few others I can't think of right now. To all of you, I say, do your best now so you won't have any regrets tomorrow.

To my family and friends, I simply say thank you. You all have been supportive of me and this dream I have. I love each and every one of you.

Oh, I have to thank this person, Mr. Christopher Little, head counselor at Stephenson High School in Stone Mountain, GA. Yeah, I'm calling you out...lol. For everything you do, I truly appreciate you.

To my publisher and my friend, Zane. I know I stressed you and Charmaine both with the delivery of this book. (sorry) Thank you for the opportunities and for keeping me in your circle.

To the husband, Warren. Thank you for working hard so I don't have to. At least not for someone else... lol. I appreciate all that you do, even though sometimes I don't act like it. After 20 years, you'd think you would know me by now...lol

I had one of my little cousins (I know you're 28, Twyla, but you'll always be my lil' cousin) ask me if I would consider not making the ending of this story a happy one. I told her I would think about it and I thought about it the entire time I wrote this story. Then I realized something. I write happy endings because *I* like them. It's the reason why I fell in love with reading. For some it's an escape from all the crap they might be going through in their lives. I know people like to say we are a work in progress, but some of us may need a little hope. So, for any of you in need, this happy ending and every other one I write is for you.

About the Author

Shonda Cheekes is a former freelance publicist and Strebor Books author of *Another Man's Wife* and *In the Midst of It All*; as well as short stories anthologized in the bestselling *Blackgentlemen.com* and *Breaking the Cycle*. She lives in the Metro Atlanta area with her husband and two children.

Book Discussion Guide

❏ If you could, would you hire a company like DeCoys to investigate your significant other?

❏ Did you think Deeva should've told Tristan about her business or kept it to herself like she did?

❏ Do you think Deeva was wrong for not telling Tristan about Octavia wanting to have him investigated?

❏ Do you think Deeva should've left Tristan alone after Octavia came into her office, or was she right for following her heart?

❏ What did you think about Fallon and Lorenzo?

❏ What did you think about Quincy?

❏ What did you think about the situation with Deeva and her mother?

❑ What do you think about the way Deeva handled the situation with Lisa?

❑ Would you have forgiven Tristan for the episode in the club?

❑ What did you think about Deeva using the information she had about Lorenzo?